MW00424435

Snow in Love

Libby Kay

Snow in Love
Copyright © 2022 Libby Kay
All rights reserved.

ISBN: (ebook) 978-1-958136-22-5
(print) 978-1-958136-23-2

Inkspell Publishing
207 Moonglow Circle #101
Murrells Inlet, SC 29576

Cover art by: Fantasia Frog Designs
Edited by: Yezanira Venecia

DEDICATION

To my husband, who never stops supporting me
or my writing dreams.
Love you, Curly.

LIBBY KAY

CHAPTER ONE

Connor Shoemaker squeezed his eyes shut. If he tried hard enough, perhaps the nightmare would dissipate. Maybe if he held his breath he could stay in the present, tangled in his sheets and drenched in sweat. But it was not going to be that easy, because this wasn't some run-of-the-mill bad dream. He wasn't a child, and his parents wouldn't burst through the door to hold him while he came back to real life. No, this was the most painful moment of his life playing on repeat in his brain like a double-feature matinee. He gave up on sleep, tossing the blankets to the side and stumbling from bed. He knew he should put on his prosthetic leg, but with his head in a fog, he couldn't focus.

Hopping out to the kitchen, Connor poured a glass of water and leaned against the cool, marble countertop. Despite the change of scenery and cold drink, he couldn't shake the remnants of his dream. The sound of scraping metal, the feel of warm blood seeping through his tracksuit, the churn in his gut that told him life was never going to be the same; it all felt as real now as it did three years ago. Connor downed the rest of the water and wiped his mouth with the back of his hand.

Glancing around his condo, he searched in vain for

something to divert his attention. He needed something—anything—to pull him from the past. In moments like this, Connor knew he needed a pet. Surely a dog or cat would know how to comfort him. Animals were loyal; they stayed when things got tough. Unfortunately for him, human companionship was in short supply since his accident.

The space around him was dark, save for the blue flashing light of his cell phone. He'd forgotten it last night, left on its charging cradle. The early hour didn't stop him from checking the waiting text message, and he groaned when he saw it. This wasn't the distraction he wanted right now.

I'm serious, Con. Be at the lodge by the 18th. Training starts when the sun comes up. — km.

The text was from Karl Masters, one of the best alpine skiing coaches in North America. He was known for gold medals and impractical, demanding training regimens for his athletes. He'd also been sniffing around Connor since the first time he strapped on a pair of skis.

A year after the accident that ended Connor's motocross career, he had bumped into Karl at a mixer for Paralympic athletes. When motocross was no longer an option, Connor started researching other sports. No matter what his body looked like now, he needed to chase that need for speed. He liked going fast, on and off the course. He'd earned every ounce of his bad boy reputation, and he wore it like a badge of honor. The problem now was that he wasn't much of a bad boy, or a speed demon for that matter. Karl wanted to change all that, with proper training.

The Winter Paralympic Games were months away, and Karl had his sights on sweeping the gold medals for both men's and women's alpine events. His competitive nature was known across the globe, and he'd do anything to recruit the best athletes. Even though Connor enjoyed hitting the slopes, skiing still didn't feel as comfortable as riding his bike did. His body wasn't the body he'd trained with for over a decade. Now the rules were different, and, frankly, he wasn't sure he wanted to play by them.

Grabbing his phone, Connor hobbled back to his bedroom and flopped onto the mattress. He was too awake for sleep, and he mindlessly rubbed his leg. Even after all this time, phantom twinges happened when his brain was stuck in the past. It was as if his lost limb taunted him from the beyond. "Like I need more reminders," he mumbled to himself.

He scrolled through a string of texts from Karl, promising him the competition and glory that had made him a star on two wheels. Connor had to admit, he didn't have anything keeping him home for Christmas. The idea of staying in a closed-down ski lodge on someone else's dime didn't seem half bad, and he thought he might take Karl up on the offer.

After all, what did this bad boy have to lose? He'd already lost so much.

*

Sienna Markum sat at the breakfast table, her eyes blurry and her mind racing. "What do you mean that training runs through Christmas? I thought we were going to Italy for the holidays." She sipped from her mug of green tea and frowned at her parents, who both looked prepared for a tongue-lashing from their daughter.

"We are going to Italy," her mother started, keeping her gaze on her clasped hands. "But you're not." Silently, her father nodded and shrugged. Opening his mouth a few times, he finally gave up on speaking and jerked his head in an odd mixture of a shrug and a nod. He looked like a defected bobblehead doll.

Never one to be easily deterred, Sienna stood from her perch on the kitchen stool and stalked to the sink. She poured her tea down the drain and dropped the mug into the sink. The loud thud echoed in the too-quiet kitchen. "You promised me a vacation," she accused with a finger pointed at her parents. "You promised if I won gold at nationals, I could have the holidays to rest. I need the downtime." Sienna hated the whiney tone in her voice, but she didn't want to lose the argument.

Also not one to be deterred, her mother kept her tone even. "Karl said this is the best training slope he could get right now. The lodge is closed to the public during renovations, so you'll be alone and able to focus. You are this close, Sienna"—her mother's manicured fingers pinched together, almost as tightly as Sienna's brows—"I'm not going to have you getting lazy, or God forbid fat, while you're so close to your dream."

Hoping her father would back her up, Sienna looked to him for support. "You want to spend Christmas without your only child?"

Before her father could answer, her mother interjected, "Get a grip. You're twenty-five years old. We all know you can handle one Christmas on your own." Her mother stood and left the kitchen. With an apologetic shrug, her father left close behind. So much for an ally.

Born without the bottom half of her left leg, Sienna never felt like she was missing anything. Her parents spoiled her rotten and treated her like she was a regular kid. After a fateful family trip to Vermont, Sienna had been introduced to the joys of skiing. Her parents had bought her a sled, but she hadn't been satisfied. Sienna wanted to ski; she wanted to go fast. With a few modifications, Sienna had her first set of skis and was hooked. No matter her mood, gliding down a mountain always made her smile. Nothing compared to the feel of winter air on her cheeks; it never failed to elevate her heart rate.

Sienna ran her hands through her dark hair. If she were honest with herself, she would admit she was bone-tired. The last twenty years of her life had been full of training and competition. Getting up before dawn was the routine.

Skipping parties and social engagements was normal. It was an unofficial rule in her small social circle that inviting Sienna to anything during training season was pointless. Not only couldn't she come, but if she did manage to squeak out a few hours to herself, she'd never really enjoyed herself. Competition loomed, and she had to be ready.

It was nearly impossible not to think about what-ifs when Sienna evaluated her life. She wondered what else there was to life. She was the Golden Girl of Paralympic alpine skiing, winning national and world competitions for the last decade. These were accomplishments she was proud of, that she earned with her own blood, sweat, and tears. The only prize that eluded Sienna was Winter Paralympic gold.

Of course, she wanted to win. But she also wanted to be a normal woman. A woman who had a life of her choosing, who could eat and drink what she wanted, see who she wanted, and do whatever she liked. Even something as mundane as joining a book club appealed to Sienna. But sitting idly with a book in her hands was seen as wasted time by her mother, who also happened to be her manager. Breaking away to read a paperback was not a priority in the Markum household, much to Sienna's growing disappointment.

Christmas was her favorite time of year. She loved the traditions, the escape from the normal schedules and expectations. The air smelled sweeter and the world seemed a little happier when the calendar turned to December. And within a matter of minutes, her coach and parents took it away. Sulking like a child wouldn't get Sienna her Christmas back, but for the time being it made her feel better.

Sienna walked to her bedroom and slammed the door shut, feeling satisfied with the crashing reverberation. She retrieved her laptop and searched for the Colorado lodge she was going to call home for the next month. It was a nice enough building in the foothills of Aspen. Although Karl was her new trainer, she trusted his judgment and suggestions.

A coach couldn't build a reputation like Karl's without results. Rumor had it his house had a room dedicated to his athletes' awards and accolades. And, frankly, anyone was better than her most recent coach. Vlad was as scary and tyrannical as a Russian villain from an '80s action movie. She shuddered at the thought of spending the holidays with that brute.

Yet despite the change in coaches, recently, Sienna started craving more from life. She craved normalcy and the freedom that came with being just a regular woman. The same joy wasn't there when she thought about competing, but Sienna also knew she needed to try. Devoting her life to the sport only to give up at the finish line didn't sit right with her—it didn't feel like the Sienna Markum way.

Her beloved rescue dog, Roscoe, sauntered up to her side. Clearly her emotional state was not pushing away her best friend. "You'll miss me, won't you?" Sienna rubbed behind the dog's ear and his tail wagged faster than a metronome. "Good boy," she cooed. It wasn't lost on Sienna that she was more devasted to leave her dog than her parents.

Pulling out her suitcase, Sienna began to pack. Because win or lose, she felt like her skiing career was at a turning point. She'd been under her parents' thumb as they dictated her every move for as long as she could remember. Where to train, when to sleep, what to eat, who to socialize with—it was all planned for her. Now she wanted to make her own plan.

The future was calling, and Sienna was ready to answer.

CHAPTER TWO

"Your room is going to be across the hall from mine," Karl said over his shoulder as he gestured toward a pair of heavy oak doors. The hallway was wide and had thick carpeting the color of mulled wine. With a quick turn on his heel, Karl pointed to the door next to Connor's room. He hesitated before saying, "This will be Sienna's room."

Connor raised an eyebrow. "Sienna?" He didn't realize he'd have to share Karl's time, but he wasn't complaining. Despite his struggles, Connor was a social animal at heart. Having someone else in the lodge would make training more interesting.

Karl gave Connor a skeptical look. "Sienna, as in Sienna Markum. Only one of the greatest slalom champions ever." He paused for effect, relaxing when he saw recognition flash over Connor's eyes. "This will likely be her final Paralympics, so she's trying a new training regime."

Connor smirked. "The Golden Girl." *Yeah, this just got a whole lot more interesting.*

Karl nodded.

Connor had seen enough coverage of Sienna and her career since he'd started skiing. Back when he was on the bike, he'd never paid attention to other sports. His day started and ended with bikes—and other activities that didn't take place on a track. Sienna was the face of slalom, and it was a beautiful face at that.

As if sensing what Connor was thinking, Karl raised a hand and shook his head. "Listen here, Con. You're here to ski, period. Don't get in Sienna's way, because that will surely mean getting in your own way. With or without your libido, I think we need to focus on training."

There was no point in arguing, because Connor knew Karl was right. Connor's motocross career had been filled with women, drinking, and a lot of speed. He'd curbed his drinking since the accident, which was no small feat, but the women situation cleared itself up. Few women are attracted to aging, injured former champions fighting alcoholism. But his priorities were different now.

A thud came from down the hall, and Connor assumed it was his training partner. Karl skipped ahead and clapped his hands. "Sienna, right on time."

Walking behind their coach, Connor gave himself a moment to take in the Golden Girl in person. He was not disappointed. Sienna was on the tall side, with a lean, toned frame and shiny, black hair she kept pulled into a tight ponytail. Her cheeks were flushed from carrying her bags down the hall, but the pink hue suited her features.

While he wore a standard prosthesis, Sienna opted for a blade that curved at the base. It looked fast even as she stood still. They both had below-the-knee amputations, but Connor was certain she was born that way. During one of his early competitions, he'd watched an interview of Sienna discussing her nearly two-decade-long career. Without hesitation, Sienna discussed the birth defect that shaped her life. There had almost been pride in her voice—pride Connor certainly didn't feel. She couldn't understand the loss and emotional devastation that came from losing something you took for granted.

Karl stepped back and reached his arm out toward Connor for introductions. "Connor, this is Sienna."

Turning, Karl faced Sienna and his tone grew cautious. "Connor will be training with us. He's going to do the slalom at the games, too."

At first, Sienna didn't say anything. Her cool, gray gaze swept from Karl to Connor as she gathered her thoughts. Finally, she raised an eyebrow. "My parents said this was a closed training session. I gave up my holidays for private lessons." Her voice was even, but the chill to her tone was unmistakable. This wasn't the public's Golden Girl; this was the real Sienna.

To his credit, Karl didn't flinch. "You will have private lessons. With the lodge and the slopes to ourselves, we'll have plenty of time to train."

She studied both men for a moment before finding her voice again. Her stern expression cracked into a devilish grin. She pointed at Connor with a slender finger. "You're that motocross guy, right? The 'bad boy' who's taking over the Paralympics." Her last statement was not a question, but it was a little judgmental.

Connor knew she already had his number, and he was quickly finding hers. "And you're the ice princess who can't share her coach." He crossed his arms over his broad chest and smirked. No doubt, he was going to have fun ruffling her pristine feathers.

Karl bristled and stepped between his athletes. "All right, introductions are over." He gently shoved Connor back a step and turned to Sienna. "Our session starts in one hour. I'm getting Connor started up on hill five. Meet me at the lifts to hill six. Got it?" Sienna went back into business mode and nodded once. She pulled her duffle bag over her shoulder and headed toward her room. Connor had to stop himself from turning around to watch her walk away. Suddenly, training didn't seem nearly as boring as he'd thought it would be.

*

13

Sienna tossed her bag on the floor and flopped down on her bed. She let out a long, cleansing breath and tried to stop her racing heart. Connor Shoemaker was here, and he was just as gorgeous as he was in his pictures. Sienna would be lying if she said she wasn't painfully aware of Connor, his reputation, and chiseled good looks. She'd have to be living under a mountain to miss all the press about his transition to another sport. Over the last year, he'd had nearly as much publicity as she did, and that was saying something.

When Connor broke into competitions, the media had gone wild. Always a born competitor, he'd taken to the slopes like a fish to water. Within a year of changing sports, he podiumed at four events, two of them at a national level. It was impossible for Sienna not to know who he was. During her own interviews, journalists loved asking for her opinion on him. The two were polar opposites. Connor built an entire career on making a scene. He played hard, partied hard, and from what she'd heard, he enjoyed the company of more women than she had met in her lifetime.

By comparison, Sienna was darn near virginal. Thanks to her parents, she kept her "good girl" image intact. No, she was certainly not a virgin. But she'd kept her personal life private and rarely did in-depth interviews. Everything stayed bland and civil. And as of an hour ago, it was how she'd thought she liked it.

How on earth would she train with Connor? How could she keep her focus when she was already feeling distracted from her goal? While her competitive drive used to be her compass, it was now wearing her down and making her second guess some of her choices. She couldn't find her true north, and it scared her.

There were so many things she missed while she spent months on end training, working out, and honing her craft. When she was on the slopes, her friends were getting married and starting families and careers. Sienna had no idea what waited for her when she hung up her skis, and she was both thrilled and terrified at the prospect.

A buzzing from her purse distracted her. She retrieved her cell and saw her mother's number. "Hi, Mom." She leaned back into the pillows of the plush bed. Even under construction, this place was still lush.

The background noise on the phone was loud, and she could barely hear her mother. "Sienna, we're about to board our flight. I wanted to make sure you made it to the lodge. Was Karl there?"

Sienna bit her lip, smiling at the thought that her mother was in the dark on the Connor situation. "Yes, he's here. I'm about to grab my gear and hit the slopes."

More muffled sounds through the phone drowned out her mother's voice. "Then I won't keep you. Remember, keep your eye on the prize. You're so close to our dream." Her mother hung up ... without so much as a goodbye.

Sienna wasn't sure why she was upset over missing the holidays with her parents, because they wouldn't let her do what she wanted. What she really wanted was peace and relaxation, no expectations hanging over her. Sienna craved lazy nights by the fire, with a mug of hot chocolate and dancing lights all around her. Now, as she looked around her hotel room, she thought she might at least get the peace she was looking for.

After fifteen minutes of unpacking and donning her ski gear, Sienna was out in the brisk Aspen sunlight. Drawing in a lungful of air, she got in the mindset for training. She raked her gaze across the scenery, and it was hard not to marvel at the beauty. There were six inches of fresh powder below her skis, and the sky was as blue as Connor's eyes.

Wait, where did that come from? *Sure, Connor's eyes were blue*, she thought, *but why was that coming to mind now?*

"Hey, Golden Girl!" Sienna heard Connor's voice as he slid to a halt in front of her. He used his wrist to pull up his goggles, dazzling her with said blue eyes. They literally sparkled like a character in her favorite vampire romance novel. Damn him.

Sienna bristled. "Don't call me Golden Girl. Do you

happen to see Bea Arthur around here?" Sienna assumed he wouldn't get the reference, but she wasn't that lucky.

Connor shrugged before stabbing his poles into the snow. He put his hands on his hips and said, "I'm more of a Betty White fan."

Sienna slid toward Connor and lifted her chin. "Betty seems a little too sweet for you. Aren't you more into the Blanches of the world?"

A glorious grin cracked Connor's face as he chuckled. "Nice to know you're worried about my type. Frankly, I'm surprised you have enough time to pay attention. Don't you have a daycare center to dedicate, or a puppy to rescue?"

Mentioning her beloved dog, Roscoe, brought Sienna's blood boiling. Throw in the fact that he mocked her charity work, and Connor Shoemaker was officially on her shit list. "I'll have you know, I like helping people." She hesitated, worrying her bottom lip. "And I like animals. Who doesn't love puppies? Roscoe is a very good boy." She hated how lame her argument sounded, but she wouldn't have anyone dissing her doggo.

Connor's smirk only grew. "Fair enough, sweetheart. Your golden reputation lives another day. Even I can't argue with puppies."

Before Sienna could come up with a sparkling rebuttal, Karl joined them. He skied to a smooth stop and retrieved an iPad from inside his jacket. With his poles hanging from his wrists, he frantically typed on the tablet. "Connor, I'm going to email your notes. Take a break, get something to eat, then join Sienna and me back here in two hours." He peered up through his goggles at the pair. "Do we have a problem already?"

Sienna scoffed. "Already? You were planning for this?"

Karl eyed Connor before turning his gaze to Sienna. "I haven't worked with Connor much, but let's say that both of your reputations precede you. I was afraid we'd have an oil and water situation on our hands."

"And you didn't want to upset the golden apple cart,

right?" Connor didn't seem disappointed with Karl's opinion of his reputation. In fact, it seemed to please him. "I'll go take a break. See you both later." He turned to Sienna and winked, his eyes glittering with mischief.

Sienna was proud of herself because she didn't say a thing. She also didn't let her eyes follow him as he skied down the hill. She was a professional, and she could get through a couple weeks in the company of Connor Shoemaker.

CHAPTER THREE

Unable to focus on Karl's notes, Connor paced around his room. Sienna was not what he'd expected. Yes, she was gorgeous. With large, almond-shaped eyes, dark hair the color of licorice, and a toned body that proved her dedication to the sport. She was utterly unforgettable.

And for as much of an impact as she made on him, Connor feared he was not going to change her mind on his—albeit well-earned—reputation. Yes, he had spent his motocross years in the beds of several women. He was no saint, but he was a gentleman. Everyone had a good time, and everyone left satisfied.

Here's the problem now—no one was satisfied. Once his injuries healed and Connor was back on his feet, or foot to be more accurate, he'd had a few dates. The dates had followed the tried-and-true pattern of fancy dinner and tour of his penthouse, but when they'd made it to the bedroom Connor discovered his gusto beneath the sheets was missing. Gone was the carefree bad boy. He was replaced by a man with aches and pains and scars to match his shredded mental state. Connor hadn't been *the* Connor Shoemaker since the accident, and he was tired of it.

That's why Sienna's assumption hurt so much.

Although, he hadn't been much better toward her. He'd promised himself he would be polite, earn her trust as a training partner. If the lower half of his body wanted more from their time together, he wasn't against that either. But what had he gone and done? He was rude and snarky, just like the Connor Shoemaker of yesteryear. In short, he'd blown it.

Connor decided it was time to man up and read Karl's notes. He was here to train; he was here to hone his competitive edge he'd lost when they amputated his leg. Despite his first year in the sport, he knew his success and results were mostly a fluke. Natural talent could only take him, or anyone, so far. There were younger guys who had trained for a decade and were ready to push Connor off the podium.

Zipping up his coat, Connor was ready for round two with Sienna. Once he was outside, he felt how calm his surroundings were. Where motocross was known for dirt, loud crowds, and the screech of engines, Alpine skiing was all about pristine landscapes and relative quiet. The one big surprise for Connor had been how much he'd grown to prefer the quiet.

"Right on time, I like that." Karl slapped Connor's back as the three skied together. "Did you have a chance to look over my notes? I'd like us to work on your turns and mind your bombing."

Sienna pulled an electrolyte tube from her pocket and sipped it wearily. Connor could tell she was waiting for him to say something inappropriate. He would not rise to the occasion. "Sounds good, Karl. I'm ready to work." He pulled down his goggles and skied toward the lift.

A few minutes later, the trio stood at the top of one of the biggest hills at the site. It was very similar to what he and Sienna would see in competition, and Connor smiled to himself. His adrenaline ramped up; the competitor inside him roared. It was time to go fast.

Karl gestured to a curve in the slope before turning to

Sienna. "Sienna, you're going to go first. Stay on the edge, and watch out for the crud at the right side of the turn. You hit that at the wrong angle, and you're flat on your ass." Turning his attention to Connor, Karl continued, "You're going to follow Sienna and do what she does. Sounds good?"

Sienna looked uncomfortable, but didn't argue. "Anything special you want me to do, Karl?"

Shaking his head, Karl waved off her question. "You're very controlled. What I'm trying to teach Connor is control. You're a master at it." In terms of skiing, that was a mega compliment, but Connor saw from the fall of Sienna's face that it was more of an insult. This shift in her fascinated him. What was that expression hiding?

And just like that, she got into her version of competitor mode. Sienna perched on the edge ready to go. "Try to keep up, huh?" she suggested over her shoulder. Connor was intrigued, but he wouldn't let her see it. Instead, he would focus. If his gaze happened to drift to her amazing backside, then there was nothing he could do about it.

As it turned out, Connor didn't have time to watch Sienna's backside. She was fast as lightning as she turned and glided down the slope with the ease of a seasoned champion. He was nearly out of breath before they were halfway down the hill. Behind him, Connor heard Karl shouting orders, but he couldn't hear through the racing beats of his heart. It was the adrenaline of the ride, but also being this close to Sienna in action. It was truly a sight to behold.

Sienna slid to a stop at the base of the hill, barely a hair out of place. "Sorry you couldn't keep up," Sienna greeted Connor as he came to a stop. She arched a manicured eyebrow at him. "You probably would have, if you weren't ogling my ass."

Before he could stop himself, Connor blurted out the first thing that came to mind. "You're incredible."

He could tell his words caught her off guard, as she

frowned slightly. "Excuse me?"

"I said, you're incredible." He edged closer on his skis and took in the flush of her cheeks and the fire in her eyes. Sienna looked alive out here. "Sure, I've seen footage of you in competition, but never like this. You were just having fun, and it was amazing to watch." Being the man he was, Connor wondered what other physical pursuits she excelled at, but he stifled his libido.

Sienna kept her gaze lowered and backed away from Connor and his praise. "Let's see what Karl has to say." She was gone before he could respond.

And yet again, this Golden Girl surprised Connor. For someone who'd lived in the limelight her whole life, she certainly didn't seem to like praise. What bothered him was that he wanted to know why.

*

Sienna felt off when she met Connor and Karl in the dining room that evening. She came down in her standard post-training outfit of yoga pants and an oversized sweater. The muffled voices of both men echoed in the empty dining space, and she took a moment to look at her temporary home.

It looked like a ski lodge from a movie set, with exposed wooden beams, a roaring fireplace and a dozen beheaded mammals studded across the walls. In the far corner by the fireplace was a scene that warmed Sienna's heart: a Christmas tree. While not grand for the space it was in, it was tastefully decorated with red ribbons, white lights, and silver ornaments. Without her permission, her feet propelled her toward it. Savoring a moment of holiday peace, she cupped one of the ornaments in her hand. A tender smile crossed her face.

"That's a side of the Golden Girl we don't always get to see," Connor's voice boomed from the far side of the room. He walked up to her and flashed his charming grin. She felt her stomach tighten as their eyes met.

"What side is that?" she asked, crossing her arms and trying not to drown in his blue gaze. Eyes like that should be outlawed—or at least come with a warning. *Danger! Risk of drowning if you're within ten yards of Connor Shoemaker's eyeballs!*

Connor shrugged, completely disarmed. "A content, happy Sienna." She raised an eyebrow in question, so he continued. "I saw you walk in and head straight for that tree." He hitched his thumb over his shoulder, and she couldn't help but see how soft his manly features looked in the dim lighting. Outside he was all masculine lines in the sunshine, but here he was in soft-focus. It was like the man walked around with a personal lighting crew. "You looked so happy, so peaceful. It was nice." He shrugged, as if his words hadn't hit their mark.

Well, she certainly didn't have a cutting reply for his remark. Plus, he seemed genuine. "Thanks. I'm just relieved to see a Christmas tree here. I was afraid they wouldn't bother with one."

"They didn't, but I made sure they would," Karl said from the doorway. "When I talked to your parents, they said that this was a very important time of year for you." He pulled from a bottle of beer and seemed totally at home in the lodge. His gray sweater looked so thick, Sienna was tempted to poke his chest and see if he'd feel it. Despite working outside most of the time, he was known for being cold no matter the location.

Sienna's mouth watered at the beer. "Any chance you have an extra one of those around? I'll skip carbs with dinner if I can have a beer." She clasped her hands in front of her, and both Karl and Connor laughed.

"Golden Girl, you continue to surprise me." Connor's smile had her palms sweating and her mind racing in naughty directions.

Fortunately, Karl was ready to insert himself into her rambling thoughts. "One beer, but only after we go over the training plan for tomorrow."

Everyone agreed and headed for their table.

Just as she eased down in her seat, a waiter arrived with a plate of steamed vegetables and grilled fish. She tried not to let her disappointment show when Connor pulled a plate of pasta toward him. "I shouldn't have promised my carbs if I'd known there weren't any to barter with," she scoffed when the waiter walked away.

Karl had the manners to look slightly embarrassed. "Your mother sent your menu requirements ahead of time. Next week I'll have the staff make some changes."

Of course her mother had sent over a strict menu. Last week Sienna had been caught with a Snickers bar in her bedroom. There probably would have been less chaos if she were found naked in bed with the cast of the Avengers. "It's not your fault." Sienna pierced a carrot with her fork and bit it in half. If she closed her eyes, she might be able to pretend it was mac and cheese or a nice roasted potato. *Yeah, right.*

When she opened her eyes, she saw Connor studying her. "Why don't we get those beers now? I think both Sienna and I deserve a little treat after today." Lowering his voice, he leaned closer and added, "and I need to see you consume more than a hundred calories for dinner."

Sienna couldn't help herself; she chuckled. "That would be a welcome distraction."

Karl rose from his seat and stretched. "I'll get a couple beers. You two confirm your schedules for tomorrow."

As soon as Karl was out of sight, Connor slid a few scoops of noodles onto Sienna's plate. "You worked your ass off today, and I'll be damned if I watch you starve while I stuff my face."

The gesture meant so much because it was exactly what Sienna wanted. Real food to support her training. Her throat closed as she tried to share her thanks. "Thank you—this is very sweet."

Connor shrugged off her praise and tucked into his own meal. He pointed at her plate with his fork and said, "You better get eating. I don't want Karl reporting back to your parents that I'm a bad influence." He winked, but sadly his joke wasn't far from the truth. Her mother would literally combust if she saw her daughter drinking a light beer while eating pasta.

Karl returned with their drinks, and the trio fell into conversation about the rest of the week's training. After an hour, Karl excused himself. Connor slowly rose to his feet and looked around the deserted room. "It's almost kind of creepy, you know? It's basically us with a few staff. Stephen King could set a hell of a book here."

Sienna was used to this type of life, with limited socializing. She supposed it was different from what Connor was used to. "I'm guessing motocross is different?"

Connor thoughtfully rubbed the stubble on his jawline. "This is definitely quieter." His fingers scratched his skin lazily, and her eyes couldn't help but follow the motion. She was mesmerized by the shape of his full lips. She allowed herself the brief fantasy of tasting those lips, of savoring the feel of them against her own. It had been a while since she'd been with a man—in any capacity—and suddenly she felt restless.

A moment later, Connor was snapping his fingers in front of her face. "Huh?" she asked, hoping he didn't notice her staring at his mouth—or the trail of drool sliding down her chin. *Real smooth, Sienna.*

He laughed. "I asked if you wanted to walk around the lodge with me. You know, explore our new digs." Connor looked relaxed, his hands shoved in his pockets. Sienna knew if she went back to her room already her evening would be dull. She'd find a rerun of *Law and Order* to watch while she combed through her training notes and did some yoga poses. There wasn't anything wrong with that plan, but it felt painfully boring.

Before she could think of a real reason to go back to her room, she shrugged and followed her gut. "I'd love to." Sienna couldn't be certain, but she felt like the smile Connor gave her was a real one—one reserved just for her.

CHAPTER FOUR

To say Connor was surprised by Sienna's willingness to join him would be a gross understatement. The only thing more surprising was that he asked at all. Their dinner with Karl had been uneventful, but her demeanor was not what Connor had expected. When she was dressed down to her basic self, she seemed so much more approachable. The fact that she took some of his proffered pasta sealed the deal for him. Sienna Markum was hungry in more ways than one.

Connor had only been at the lodge a few hours longer than Sienna, but he'd used the time wisely and snooped around the lower level. The west wing was closed off behind sheets of plastic, with the interior rooms already gutted. He didn't mind the mismatch of a construction zone and a deserted hotel. It was actually kind of fun.

"I don't know what's going to be unlocked, but the map of this place seems pretty cool." He pulled a brochure for the lodge out of his back pocket and handed it to Sienna. Because he couldn't help himself, he let their fingers graze each other before pulling back. Connor's traitorous body reacted to the brief touch, zipping a charge up his spine. He could feel himself blush and felt like an awkward teenager trying to steal a goodnight kiss.

If Sienna noticed the contact, she didn't react. Connor told himself it was for the best. The last thing either of them needed this close to the games was complications. She frowned as she peered at the map. "It says they have a pool. I should have brought my suit." Her bottom lip jutted out in a pout that Connor had to look away from. If he focused too long on that plush skin, he'd do something foolish.

A million dirty thoughts ran through his mind. Skinny-dipping with the beautiful, shapely woman next to him was one good way to spend a cold, lonely evening. As if she read his mind, Sienna laughed. "I can almost hear the gears turning in that head of yours." She reached up and gently flicked his forehead. The casual, yet intimate, gesture felt like someone had thrown him into another dimension.

Women never teased Connor, not unless he started it. He loved that Sienna was getting under his skin already. If nothing else, it would keep the next few weeks entertaining. "What makes you think I was thinking anything untoward?" He splayed his hand across his chest in mock horror. "You offend me, madam."

A giggle escaped Sienna's stern expression, and it was like music for his soul. "Well, I'm just going by your reputation. Rumor has it you've had plenty of opportunities for illicit swimming in your day."

In his day. The words were said in jest, but Connor suddenly felt sick to his stomach. Granted, he made his reputation one bad decision at a time. He wasn't necessarily sorry about his past, because life didn't give time for regret. But for some reason, he wanted Sienna to see him for who he was in that moment. A man who was more vulnerable than he wanted to admit.

Rubbing the lump in his chest, Connor tried to laugh off her comment as they walked down a deserted hallway toward the pool. "Let's say that my reputation didn't follow me to skiing. My partying days are over." The words were true, and they didn't terrify him as much as they used to. Sharing this truth with Sienna didn't feel scary; it felt right.

Sienna caught up to him as he pulled the door open to the pool room. It was unlocked, and the door creaked as it opened. It sounded like a sound effect from a Vincent Price movie. "Creepy," she whispered. She was so close he felt the warmth and proximity of Sienna. He wasn't sure if he could be this close and not have an awareness of her. Leaning closer as they crept inside the pool room, he caught a whiff of her shampoo. It was light and citrusy, like a glass of lemonade on a summer's afternoon.

"Let me get my phone out," she whispered, fumbling with the flashlight app.

Before Connor could offer his help, the light from her phone blazed a beam into the large, dark space. "Watch your step," he warned as she stepped ahead to investigate. He stayed close behind her, struggling to see much beyond stacks of chairs and an empty towel rack.

Sienna inched forward and stopped right before the edge of the pool, her prosthesis scraping on the tiled floor. "No swimming for us, clothed or otherwise. There hasn't been water in this pool in a while." The light from her phone shone on the dry, cracked concrete base. The surface was as parched as the Mojave Desert in August.

Connor stood still, battling with the image of them naked in this private oasis. After seeing Sienna in her leggings, it didn't take much imagination to fill in the blanks. His fingers itched with the need to reach out and touch her, to fall into her arms and bask in her warmth. *God, he needed to get a grip.*

"I won't lie, Golden Girl, that is disappointing."

Even in the darkness, he felt Sienna tense in front of him. "Didn't think I had it in me, huh?"

Connor shrugged. "I guess we're both preceded by our reputations."

The words hit their intended mark and Sienna spun around to face him. "And just what does that mean?" Her gray eyes sparkled in the dim room, and Connor knew they were filled with fire. "You don't know anything about me."

Connor crossed his arms over his chest and stuck out his chin. He was raring for a fight; he felt his blood pumping. Whether it was adrenaline or being so close to Sienna, he was hot. "And what makes you think you know me? We only just met."

Hesitating a moment, Sienna blinked through the dim lighting. "Then let's agree that neither of us knows anything about the other person. Deal?" One hand still clutching her cell phone, Sienna offered Connor the other to shake.

"Fine, Golden Girl. Let's start over." He reached out to take her hand, and time stopped. A jolt of awareness shot through him, all the way down to his prosthesis. A small gasp escaped Sienna's mouth, which he hoped meant she felt the heat between them, too. Allowing the moment to linger, he gently tugged her closer. Sienna took a wobbly step forward. Savoring the weight of her hand in his, he swept his thumb over her knuckles. He didn't miss the way she shuddered in response. Sienna's skin was delectably soft, like marshmallows in a mug of hot chocolate. *God, he really needed to get a grip. He was starting to wax poetic.*

Sienna pulled back, her arm dropping to her side. "We should probably go to bed. Uh, I mean … our own beds." Her stammer brought a chuckle from Connor, and he definitely felt validated. He hadn't made a woman tongue-tied in way too long, and it felt damn good.

Ever the gentleman, Connor stepped to the side and gestured for Sienna to exit first. "Ladies first," he said.

With one eye on Connor and the other on her phone, Sienna wasn't watching for the strips of carpet that were already peeling. Her blade slid under a carpet tile, and she lost her footing. As she lurched forward, Connor sprang ahead and caught her by her forearms. The momentum caused them to both fall on the floor, with Sienna landing on top. He tensed and absorbed most of the impact.

A rush of air escaped her lungs as she lay sprawled on top of Connor. Neither one of them spoke as they caught their breath. Unable to let her go, he braced her by the hips.

"Are you okay?" he asked, his voice an octave lower than normal. His body was painfully aware of her weight on top of him.

Sienna made no attempt to get up, instead she reached toward his face and with the tips of her fingers, gently swept a loose curl. They smiled at each other, eyes locking with only the beam of her discarded cell phone around them.

Connor's fingers tensed on her hips as her gaze lowered from his eyes to his mouth. Any sliver of self-control he had evaporated as Sienna sighed. The feel of her breath on him was too much to bear. "Can I?" he breathed the question, hoping she was on the same page. Lifting his chin, he closed the space between them and kissed her gently on the lips. The kiss was tender, and he felt something inside him click for the first time in three years.

Teasing, his tongue slipped out to part Sienna's lips. At first, she reciprocated, moaning into his mouth and tugging on his hair. He felt the strands pull at his scalp, but he didn't mind. All his attention was fixated on her lips—delectable pillows he wanted to savor all night.

Then as soon as it had started, Sienna pulled back and staggered to standing. He missed her and tried not to crumble at the sight of her fumbling to break free. "I'm sorry, I ..." She covered her face with one hand and reached for her fallen phone with the other. "I should go."

Before Connor could sit up and respond, Sienna was gone. He sat on the floor in the dark for what felt like an eternity. There was a stirring in his chest, a tension in his gut that hadn't been there for ages. He wasn't naive enough to think one kiss from skiing's Golden Girl would be enough to bring back his mojo, but he was starting to think he needed to spend more time with Sienna. The only question was, did she feel the same way?

*

Control. Sienna's life was all about control, and in that

moment with Connor she'd lost every ounce of it. Pacing in her bedroom, she ran through their encounter dozens of times. The feel of his lips on hers was a surprise, to say the least. No, she did not expect to kiss him, but she wasn't going to lie and tell herself she didn't enjoy it.

Enjoying would be an understatement. That moment was one she planned to play on a loop in her brain for the rest of her life. A girl doesn't forget a kiss like that. With her exes, Sienna had felt excitement; knew what it meant to see stars in bed. Yet somehow with Connor, a kiss in an abandoned pool house had her feeling restless in ways she had never experienced. She wanted more of Connor—both on the slopes and off.

Now the question was, what did that mean?

A trilling beep alerted Sienna to an incoming call from her mother. She glanced at the time on her phone, realizing it was nearly midnight, meaning it was early morning in Italy. "Mom? Is everything okay? How's Daddy?" The uncertainty of the call brought her pulse back up, but for far less satisfying reasons. A million horrible scenarios played through her mind until her mother finally chimed in.

"Sienna? Can you hear me?" Her mother sounded worlds away, which Sienna knew she was. Italy could have been on Mars for how different it was from training. Her parents were sampling the best wine and food in Europe, and Sienna was grateful for a spoonful of pasta at dinner. The shrillness of her mother's voice brought Sienna back to the moment. "Why did you answer? You should be sleeping."

The accusatory tone was not new, and Sienna had to stifle a groan. "Mom, you called me. Of course I'm going to answer." She plopped down on the edge of her bed, reaching down with her free hand to rub her knee above her prosthesis. A day on the slopes always made the skin a little tender, even after years of training.

Willfully not picking up on her daughter's annoyance, her mother continued. "I'm calling to see how day one went.

How's Karl? Is the lodge up to your standards? They didn't screw up the menu I requested, did they? Are you hydrating enough? What about the mattress; are you sleeping?"

Sienna bristled. Even though she was in her mid-twenties, she couldn't pick her own dinner. She also couldn't be trusted to make herself comfortable. What did her mother expect to do from Italy? The micromanaging wasn't new, but how Sienna felt about it was. She was exhausted down to her core, and all she wanted to do was hang up and bury herself under the duvet. "Everything is fine. Look, it's late. I should probably get to bed."

"You haven't gone to bed yet? Isn't it nearly midnight there?" The concern in her mother's voice was undeniable, but Sienna didn't feel like it was concern of a mother. This was more the ridicule of a manager.

"Yes, it is. And if you wouldn't have called this late, I would be sound asleep." It was a lie, but Sienna knew her mother wouldn't pick up on the reason her daughter couldn't sleep. Hopefully, her mother didn't know that Connor was even at the lodge, let alone her training partner. That was a heap of trouble Sienna wasn't looking for.

Sniffing, her mother carried on with her point. "I called planning to leave a message. Your father and I are going on a vineyard tour today, and I might not have cell reception."

It didn't escape Sienna's notice that her parents were still taking the vineyard tour she had picked. There was nothing better than a robust glass of red after a long week of training, and she'd become quite the wine snob over the last two years. Granted, that beer tonight had been a welcome treat, but Sienna was a wine girl through and through. If she wasn't so disappointed in missing the tour, she could almost laugh at the thought of her mother watching strangers spit fifty-year-old wine into plastic tubs. Even though she wasn't a lush, being wasteful wasn't her mother's style.

Sienna crawled back on her bed, nestled among the pillows. Her fingers flexed with the need for a glass of wine to dull the ache of disappointment. "Look, I'm going to call it a night. Thanks for checking in." She pinched the bridge of her nose, hoping the phone call was nearing its conclusion. Her mother had a tendency to drag out conversations when she smelled blood in the water.

"All right, Sienna. You know what you need to perform. Drink plenty of water, and let me know how day two goes."

Sienna wasn't worried about her training at the moment, which was probably the real reason her mother was checking in. "Tell Daddy I said hi," she said instead.

Ignoring her daughter's comment, her mother plowed ahead with her point. "Keep your eye on the prize, eat light, and we'll get that gold before you know it." The click of the call ending was the only goodbye Sienna got.

With a flick of her wrist, Sienna tossed her phone to the nightstand and covered her face with her arm. The day had been a surprise in more ways than one, and she'd be lying to herself if she didn't admit she liked having Connor at the lodge. If nothing else, he would keep things interesting. Plus, she had a feeling she was only scratching the surface of what he was like. He came across as gruff and confident, but she felt like there was a tenderness that not everyone saw. The trouble was, she wanted to be one of the people who really knew him, and that was more terrifying than the highest ski slope.

CHAPTER FIVE

"You're at training camp with Sienna Markum? You lucky dog." Connor's brother's voice boomed through his Bluetooth speaker. Colby was almost a decade younger, recently graduated from college with a degree in political science and no desire to use it. All he wanted to do was tinker with bikes.

Connor studied his tired expression in the mirror and decided against shaving. He needed to focus on the slopes, not his five o'clock shadow. "Colby, we're sharing the same coach. This isn't *Too Hot To Handle*. We're not about to hook up." *Although wouldn't that be amazing?*

He hated that he spilled the beans to Colby about Sienna being at the lodge, as he was a dog with a bone when it came to women.

"Dude, you're a fool if you don't hit that. Skiing's Golden Girl is with you at a private ski lodge? You're living every guy's fantasy."

"Calm down. We just met."

Scoffing, Colby wouldn't let him off the hook. "The Connor I know would have slept with her and the housekeeper by now. What's up with you?" The clunking of metal echoed through the phone, and Connor pictured his brother covered in grease working on a new bike. Colby, the owner of his own garage, spent every waking moment surrounded by bikes. Motocross was still pumping through his veins.

Even just a few months ago, Colby's connection to the sport would have bothered Connor. As the older brother, he'd introduced Colby to motocross when he was barely through puberty. When Connor started hitting his stride with skiing, he knew he could start to let go of the sport that meant so much. Yes, motocross had taken away part of his leg, but it was still the reason he had a nice condo to go home to and enough money to send home to his brother, which Colby saved to help open his garage. Therapy had taught Connor to focus on what he'd gained, not just what he'd lost.

"Maybe I'm growing up, man. You should try it." Connor chuckled at the sound of Colby snorting with laughter. This was their regular banter, and it did Connor some good to feel like the teasing older brother. It felt a hell of a lot better than playing the role of victim—of survivor. Even though everyone was moving on with their lives, he'd never be able to get the image of Colby by his bedside in the hospital from his mind's eye. That was a level of heartache that no one should have to suffer through, especially a younger brother.

While Connor was impressed with his brother's determination to make motocross his life, he still worried that the sport would take over Colby's life like it did his own. His brother's blasé attitude about women wasn't new, but it was really starting to bother Connor. Although he couldn't blame Colby, he wanted to be a better example. Connor knew he wasn't always a role model before, or at least not the role model his brother deserved.

Oblivious to his brother's musings, Colby persisted in his argument. "Don't you both have a matching set?"

Misunderstanding the question, Connor laughed. "Nah, I'm pretty sure Sienna's a chick." His mind flashed back to last night's kiss, and he had to stifle a moan. She was definitely all woman—firm muscle, perfect breasts and lips that left him breathless. Right now he'd give just about anything for five more minutes in that pool house. Even if all he did was relish the weight of Sienna on top of him, Connor knew it would be time well spent. This was different. Sienna was different. Hell, he was different. There was real chemistry between them, and it felt strong enough to melt the periodic table.

Still unaware of his brother's musings, Colby sighed like the petulant younger brother he was. "I mean, aren't you both missing the same leg?"

Colby's question was innocent enough, but it caused Connor's blood to run cold. He hated talking about his injury, even if it was just with Colby. Like a tiny ember, a part of Connor burned to go back in time to the one day when he lost control of his bike.

A lump formed in his throat, and Connor knew he was on the precipice of emotions he wanted to keep buried. Besides, if he got weepy on the phone with Colby, he'd never hear the end of it. "I gotta get to the slopes. Thanks for calling." Connor stalked toward his pile of gear and snatched his skis.

Colby didn't respond right away, sensing he said the wrong thing. "Sure, dude. You do you. Hang in there."

Connor thanked him and disconnected. He needed to get out on the slopes and clear his head. Between a restless night's sleep with his favorite recurring nightmare, to replaying the kiss with Sienna, his head was not in the game—it barely felt connected to his body.

Having skipped breakfast in favor of room service, Connor hoped to avoid Sienna and any potential awkwardness this morning. Throwing his bag over his shoulder, he headed toward the lobby. His plans of avoidance ended abruptly when he saw Sienna lounging on a chair next to the Christmas tree.

She hadn't seen him come in, which gave him the

opportunity to study her in the morning light. Her legs were curled under her, supporting an iPad that she scrolled through, deep in concentration. The light caught a few strands of dark hair, making them seem almost blue. Her lips were the color of bubble gum, and Connor needed to swallow hard before he could bring himself to walk on.

"Ah, there you two are," Karl greeted them both from the lobby entrance. "I love it when my athletes are early risers." He clapped his hands and beamed at them.

Sienna kept her gaze focused on Karl. "Good morning." She smiled, but it didn't reach her eyes. Connor noticed she looked as tired as he felt, purple smudges shadowing her otherwise bright face. A smug part of him hoped their kiss had kept her up as well. He couldn't be the only lovesick fool in his situation, could he?

If Karl sensed the tension between them, he didn't show it. Instead, he turned to Connor and pointed toward the exit. "Get to the slopes, Con. I'll meet you at hill six in ten minutes. We're going to go through some new drills, then Sienna will join us before her session at eleven." Turning on his heel, he faced Sienna. "That gives you the morning to review your notes and hit the gym. Sounds good?" Rising from her chair, she nodded and turned toward the hallway, which led to a small gym.

A morning in the sun with fresh powder under his skis was exactly what Connor needed. Before he realized the time, Sienna skied up to him and Karl, a puff of snow framing her as she slid to a stop. Even these simple motions looked effortless, and Connor envied her comfort level on skis. He wondered what it was like to feel comfortable in your body like that. Would he be as graceful if he'd never had his leg in the first place? Maybe he'd get the courage to ask her about it sometime.

Karl retrieved a water bottle and slurped for a second, like he was the one skiing his ass off. Connor took the chance to move closer to Sienna. "Good morning," he greeted her with his favorite charming smile. Unfortunately, it didn't have the effect he was hoping for. She merely raised a shoulder and turned toward Karl.

"What's the plan, Karl?" she asked, motioning toward the edge of the slope with her pole. Connor knew it was a big deal that she spent time working on his training, and he planned to thank her for that later.

Before excusing himself to take a call, Karl shared their plan for the rest of the morning. This left the pair alone with nowhere to hide. Judging from the longing look Sienna was giving the mountain, Connor was pretty certain she wanted to ski to safety, or right into an avalanche.

Connor leaned closer, so only Sienna could hear him. "Are we ever going to talk to each other?" She didn't respond at first, so he pressed on. "Because it's going to be a long couple of weeks. Especially since we're the only people here." Punctuating his point, he gestured with his ski pole to the abandoned slopes around them.

"We're not alone. Karl is here."

Connor chuckled. "So, we're going to use Karl as an intermediary? I don't think he'd put up with that crap." Suddenly, a thought popped into his head. "I didn't offend you, did I? I know I was eager last night, and I'm sorry if I overstepped." Stabbing his poles into the snow, he faced her and frowned. "I hope I didn't upset you. God, Sienna. That is the last thing I want."

Watching Sienna for a reaction, Connor let out a sigh when she shook her head and met his gaze. "I wanted to"— her voice was barely a whisper—"kiss you. You didn't do anything I didn't want."

On an exhale, Connor let a slew of obscenities fly. "That's a relief," he continued when he ensured she truly wasn't cross with him. "If you're interested, I'd be more than willing to pick up where we left off." Connor winked, and he focused on the flush creeping up Sienna's cheeks. Her eyes narrowed, and he couldn't help but feel smug satisfaction as her lips quirked into a semi-smile. "Why, my goodness, is that Sienna Markum smiling at me?" Craning his neck to see her face, he exclaimed, "I believe she is!"

Sienna rolled her eyes but didn't hide her smile. "All right, I'm sorry. We can talk."

In jest, Connor took a small bow. "Thank you, madam. I promise to converse appropriately." She swatted him with her gloved hand, and being this close to her brought his blood pressure rising. Seeing that Karl was still immersed in his phone call, Connor tested the waters. "Are we going to talk about last night?"

Whether it was the cold weather or memories of their kiss, Sienna's cheeks turned crimson. "What is there to talk about?"

Connor shrugged, but he felt anything but casual. "I don't know, but it felt pretty electric to me." He hoped she felt the same way, and that was why she was playing hard to get.

"It was nice," she mumbled, head tucked toward her chest.

Connor's former mojo was back and ready to play with Sienna. He nearly fainted with relief as their flirting continued. It was like he was a tourist in a foreign land and remembered the basic questions to get where he needed to go. You know, like the post office or train station—or inside Sienna's bedroom.

"Nice? It certainly felt hot to me." Hot was an understatement; Connor had felt super-charged with her in his arms.

Sienna's pupils dilated, and her gaze swept up to his lips before darting away. "It was a mistake; we can't do it again." Her tone was firm, but she grimaced as she said the words.

"Why not? We're both adults, and Lord knows we'll have the time while we're here. Why don't we explore this connection we seem to have?" He reached out and tucked a strand of dark hair behind her ear. Sienna didn't shy away from the gesture, and that bolstered his resolve. "Have a drink with me tonight."

His offer shook her from her thoughts, and Sienna

inched back from him. "We shouldn't. We're here to train. The games are only a couple months away."

Before he could continue his argument, Karl was back. "Sorry, it was my wife. I ..." He trailed off without finishing his thought. Instead, he barked out a new set of instructions.

Connor knew it was time to get back to work, but that didn't mean he would stop pursuing Sienna. There was something about this Golden Girl, an electricity between them. They had sparked last night. He wanted to explore it because he wasn't afraid to get burned.

*

This was not a date. Sienna rested her hand over her rapidly beating heart, trying to catch her breath. She'd taken way too much time getting ready for dinner, and the subsequent drinks that would follow. Her trusty yoga pants were still there, but she paired them with a slouchy sweater that hung off her shoulder in a periwinkle that brought out the blue-gray in her eyes.

Even if this was a date, which it wasn't, Sienna felt foolish for feeling so flustered. Over the years she'd been on numerous dates with all sorts of men. Well, maybe not all sorts. Most of her boyfriends had been somehow connected to her parents. They all came from solid, wealthy families who had worked with her father over the years. She'd had some fun, but nothing like what she shared with Connor. If a simple kiss had gotten under her skin this much, she was both excited and terrified for their time alone. And she couldn't deny how much fun she had flirting with Connor. Their teasing was quickly becoming her favorite hobby.

Sienna joined Karl and Connor at the dining table, where they were both in the middle of a training discussion. Connor pointed at Karl with his fork, the gesture filled with frustration. "What are you saying, Karl? Should I pack up and go back to the Blue Runs?"

Karl slowly put down his napkin, his jaw set. "Con, I'm telling you to watch your edges and pacing. All right?"

The scraping of Sienna's footfalls alerted the men they were not alone. Both recovered quickly, as Connor rose to pull out her chair and Karl waved down the waiter for her dinner. Yet again, a plate of lean protein with steamed vegetables was placed in front of her. As she retrieved her utensils, Sienna stifled a groan. Connor nudged her with his elbow, showing her a dinner roll under his napkin. He winked, and the gesture brought butterflies with a vengeance. The little winged beasts practically juggled chainsaws in her belly.

In an effort to focus on the real reason she was in this lodge, Sienna steered the conversation back to the slopes. Connor and Karl's banter mellowed, and by the time Karl ordered coffees, everyone was relaxed. "Will there be anything else this evening, sir?" the waiter asked Karl, looking expectantly at Connor.

Karl leaned back in his seat and patted his stomach. "I think we're good to go." Before walking away, the waiter nodded at Connor, taking what appeared to be money from his hand. Sienna raised an eyebrow, but Connor didn't look at her. Just as their conversation picked back up, Karl's phone buzzed with a series of texts. He furrowed his brow and tucked the device into his pocket. "All right, we need to talk."

His dark eyes flashed between Sienna and Connor, and it made her uneasy. "What's going on?" Sienna asked, balling her napkin in her lap. She glanced over to Connor, who seemed just as confused by the shift in tone from their coach. That either made her feel better or much worse.

To his credit, Karl seemed pained about what he was going to tell them. "It's about Christmas." As in, Sienna's favorite holiday that was only a few days away.

Stealing the words from her mouth, Connor answered first. "What about it?"

Their coffees arrived, and Karl looked at it like he

wanted it to be something stronger. "I'm leaving on Christmas Eve."

Connor didn't seem bothered by the news, merely shrugging as he poured cream into his cup. "For how long?"

Karl leaned forward, emboldened by Connor's nonchalance. "Only two days. I'll be back first thing on the 26th." He looked to Sienna and held his hands in the air, palms facing her. "I swear, I'll be back before you even have breakfast on Boxing Day."

Sienna's stomach soured, and she pushed away her coffee. "Why are you leaving?" Her tone had an edge, and she knew she sounded stern by the look on Connor's face. He didn't seem to understand why this bothered her.

Pulling his phone from his pocket, Karl placed it on the table and gestured. "My wife needs me to come home for Christmas. Both of the kids are home from college, and her parents are coming in from Canada. I told her this was important, but I need to think about family for a couple days."

Blood rushed to Sienna's ears and she stood, unwilling to listen to another word. "So, you rent this lodge and convince my parents that I don't need, or deserve, a freaking vacation? Then you leave me alone on the most important day of the year?" She tossed her napkin on the table and backed away. "I'm expecting a partial refund, Karl. I'm going to go look at our contract."

Behind her, Sienna heard chairs scraping on wood and someone calling her name, but she would not stop. The fury of the sport pulling her away from life was too strong to fight in the moment. She needed time alone.

Slamming her door shut brought the slightest feeling of victory, but Sienna knew it wouldn't be enough. She was angry, and she felt isolated. At home, she could burrow herself in bed with a pint of low-fat frozen yogurt and a bottle of wine, cocooning away from the outside world.

She paced back and forth, chewing on her nails as she tried to figure out what to do with her evening. It was too early to sleep, and she didn't feel like skiing after a whole day on the slopes. Just as she was turning on the TV, a gentle knock sounded at her door. "Go away, Karl!" she barked.

"It's not Karl," a muffled voice explained.

Sienna's cheeks flushed at the sound of Connor's voice. Reluctantly, she opened the door a crack. "What are you doing here?" She raised an eyebrow at his sheepish grin. "Did Karl send you to stop me from voiding our contract?"

Connor shook his head and stepped back slightly, holding up a bottle of wine and two glasses. "I know you're upset, so I thought I'd bring our drink to you." It was a nice bottle of merlot, her favorite. Without hesitation, she opened the door for him.

He stepped into her room and glanced around. "We literally have the same room. I don't know why, but I thought yours would be pink." It was a reference at her normal competition color, but Sienna was touched he even remembered. Their paths hadn't crossed, but she liked knowing he noticed.

Speaking of noticing, Connor's eyes dragged down her frame. "You look lovely," he said in a whisper.

This was a bad idea. The man was five feet away, and Sienna was already feeling the heat of his words, of his body so near to hers. Tucking a strand of hair behind her ear, she gestured to a small table in the corner of the room. "Why don't you set the wine down over here?"

Connor placed the bottle and glasses on the table, then turned and retrieved something from his jacket pocket. "Here." He stepped toward her and handed her a ball of fabric. Sienna opened it and realized it was a napkin hiding a pair of dinner rolls. "Thought you'd probably be hungry."

Sienna was hungry all right, but for more than carbohydrates. "Thank you," she said. Greedily, she took a bite of one of the rolls. Half of the pastry disappeared before he could blink. "These are so good."

Connor went to work opening the wine. He crossed back to her and handed her one of the glasses. Sienna had never seen anything so wonderful as the sight in front of her. Connor was dressed in jeans that hung low on his hips, a T-shirt from an old motocross sponsor, and a green jacket that made him look like a Christmas present just for her. He raised his glass to clink with hers. "To the games," he offered. Taking a sip of his wine, he grimaced slightly.

Sienna found him charming. "Not a red fan?"

Connor scratched the back of his neck. "I'm more of a beer or whiskey guy."

While he didn't like the merlot, Sienna savored her first few sips. The wine warmed her from the inside, already bringing color to her cheeks. "This is my favorite—thank you."

Their hotel rooms didn't have a lot of seating, save for the two small chairs in the corner. Connor's hulking frame would likely not be comfortable there, so Sienna walked toward her bed and sat on the edge. With a quick pat, she gestured for him to join her. He didn't hesitate.

"Do you mind me asking why the Christmas thing upset you?" Connor asked, his eyes steady on her, waiting for a reaction.

Sienna took a long sip from her glass before cradling it in her hands. Without making eye contact, she shared her feelings on training and the holidays for the first time. "I haven't had a Christmas in a while. Training is always happening in the winter, whether there's a competition or not. This year I was supposed to go to Europe with my parents, was supposed to finally have a couple weeks off to enjoy my favorite time of the year. Karl found me and my parents, telling us he had this one-of-a-kind training experience planned. My parents jumped at the idea, which they only told me about a couple days before training started." She trailed off and finished her glass, knowing it would go straight to her head with only a few bites of chicken and a dinner roll in her stomach.

Connor slowly reached out his free hand and covered hers. Sienna leaned closer and let her head rest on his shoulder, enjoying the closeness. "I'm sorry, Sienna. I can tell this is important to you." He inched over, taking the empty glass from her hand. From the corner of her eye, she watched him slug back the last of his glass before putting them both on the nightstand.

Before she could miss him, he was back at her side, pulling her close with his arm around her shoulders. "I'm sorry I wasn't overly friendly today. It's not an excuse, but I have a lot on my mind."

Shaking his head, Connor rubbed her arm and said, "Don't apologize. You're under a lot of pressure. I'm freaking out, and no one expects anything from me. I'm the goof-off guy who likes to ride bikes and party, remember? I don't have everyone watching."

Sienna felt understood by someone for the first time in a long time. This relative stranger really saw her, and he wasn't backing away from the challenge. Admitting it felt nice was too big an understatement. Sienna felt free. "Connor." Her voice came out rough as gravel, then their eyes met. She licked her lips as her gaze fell to his mouth. Just as she was about to lean toward him, her phone rang and broke the moment.

Without even looking, she knew it was her mother. Sienna dragged herself away from the bed and checked her phone. For the first time ever, she declined the call and turned her phone off. "Everything okay?" he asked.

Sienna paced back to him, reaching up to cup his cheek. "Yes, everything is more than okay." Slowly, their lips met in a gentle kiss that warmed Sienna down to her toes. Connor's grip tightened slightly, but he didn't push her. She set the pace, and it turned her on to have this type of control. Raking her fingers through his hair, Sienna deepened their kiss. Hungry for more, she leaned forward, straddling him and taking what she wanted. The feeling of his scruffy face in her hands was delicious; the contrast of softness and roughness nearly intoxicating.

For once, skiing and competition were the last things on

Sienna's mind. And she was loving it.

LIBBY KAY

CHAPTER SIX

Connor did not know if it was the wine, the news of the holidays, or their general connection, but Sienna was currently plastered to him and giving him the hottest kiss of his life. Even through layers of clothing, he felt her warm body grinding on him. The only thing he could concentrate on was the delicious friction below the belt. Yoga pants left nothing to the imagination, and the sweater was doing little in providing coverage as it slid down Sienna's shoulder. A constellation of freckles ran from her collarbone to the base of her neck. Connor made a mental note to trace those sweet little dots later, as he was currently distracted with other parts of her amazing body.

Denying the phone call seemed to light something within Sienna, and Connor had so many questions. It did not take a rocket scientist to see she was sheltered. He could see it in the little things, like her menu and the fact that she had no say on her own holiday season. It would have been so easy for Sienna to be a pampered princess, but that wasn't who she was. He saw drive and determination, both on the slopes and off.

Watching her take control was hot as hell. And speaking of taking control, Connor was afraid he would lose his in about thirty seconds. He hadn't felt this with a woman in longer than he cared to admit, and breaking the kiss took all of his willpower. Yes, he wanted to take this to the next level physically, but he wasn't done getting to know this Golden Girl.

"Sienna," he breathed, cradling her face in his hands. His fingers traced the line of her cheekbones while they both struggled to catch their breath.

"Am I doing something wrong?" she asked, gently rubbing onto his growing erection. Her pink lips were swollen from their kiss, which he was already missing. Never one to skip foreplay in the past, Connor hadn't put too much thought into kissing. It was always enjoyable, but this was different. Kissing Sienna felt like something he needed to survive—more than his favorite beer or an afternoon on the slopes. Her kisses were a necessity he couldn't live without.

"No"—he cleared his throat—"you're doing everything right. That's why I think we need to take a beat here." He couldn't believe the words coming out of his mouth. Motocross Connor would have had Sienna naked and screaming his name by now, not prying her off of his body. Truly, this was an out-of-body experience.

Sienna lowered her head, not meeting his eyes. Clearly embarrassed, she scooted to the far side of the bed. "I'm usually not so forward, I—" Her words cut off when Connor pulled her back to his side. An arm draped around her shoulders, he needed her near him while he found his words.

"Listen to me, Sienna." Using his thumb, he lifted her chin to meet his gaze. "I want to keep going, more than you know." To punctuate his point, Connor gestured to the tent he was pitching below the belt. He had a feeling if his nether regions could talk, he'd get the scolding of his life right about now. "But I also want to get to know you. Can we take our time?" Inching his thumb up to her lips, he swept it across the rosy skin.

Sienna looked incredulous. "You want to talk?"

Connor nodded, just as surprised as she was that he was taking the moral high road. Frankly, it sucked. Before pulling back his hand, he swept over her lips one more time. That's when she surprised him by biting gently on the digit, sending a bolt of pleasure through him. Through a groan, he said, "You're pushing my willpower here."

Lifting her exposed shoulder, Sienna gave a coy smile. "I know we have time, but I don't want to waste it."

Connor let out a slow stream of profanities as he pulled her back to his lips. His Golden Girl was surprising him at every turn, and he needed to touch her again. She tasted like wine and smelled like orange groves in spring. He could get lost in this woman. That's why he finally pulled away and got to his feet. "Sienna, I think we should wait."

Her face fell, but she didn't look surprised. "All right. If there's anything I know, it's self-control. I suppose we can pace ourselves." Her tone told Connor that she didn't believe her own words, and he didn't blame her. Just as he was getting his mojo back, his conscience decided to make an appearance. *Thanks for that, pal.*

Thinking back to when he actually dated, Connor decided they needed to do something beyond training and stolen kisses at the lodge. Sienna deserved to be wined and dined, or at least spoiled. Before he could overthink things, he suggested, "Let me take you out tomorrow. We'll have a real date. Dinner, talking, whatever you want to do. Just you and me."

Connor knew they were the right words to say when she finally smiled at him. "You want to take me on a date?" Her happy expression grew as his offer sunk in. "That would be nice, but what about Karl?"

Waving off her concern, Connor leaned forward and placed a tender kiss on her cheek. "Let me handle Karl, okay?"

"Okay, I trust you." She couldn't have known what her words meant to him, but they filled Connor with a sense of purpose. He wasn't a fool; he knew Sienna didn't trust just anyone. She was offering more than a night in bed. Sienna had the potential to offer him everything.

Clearing his throat, he said, "I won't let you down." In response, Sienna leaned in and pulled him into a hug. Compared to the last twenty minutes it was chaste and innocent, but he savored another opportunity to be close to her. His skin burned with the need for more, but he was not going to ruin the moment. Things were new and fragile. There was a reason he hadn't had many long-term—or even short-term—relationships. Yes, he took care of his partners' needs, but they never got to know each other beyond the physical. He needed to prove to Sienna, and himself, that he could do this right. That he could be the man she deserved.

Reaching out to the nightstand, Connor grabbed the remote and turned on the TV. Sienna didn't seem deterred by the change in their plans, instead, she leaned closer and rested her hand on his thigh. It was a sweet gesture, one that did nothing to slow his racing heart. Settling on a rerun on the gameshow channel, Connor rested his head on a stack of pillows. As he settled, a whiff of citrus tickled his nose. He was quickly becoming addicted to the smell of oranges because it was the smell of Sienna.

Connor's TV choices proved to be just what they needed. While hosts in plaid, polyester suits droned on about fabulous prizes, Connor held tightly to the prize sitting next to him. During commercial breaks the pair snuck the occasional kiss, but overall, it was a PG-rated evening. He could not remember a night spent with a woman that didn't end with orgasms and hastily rumpled clothes. And the thing that terrified him most was that he was having a wonderful time. He watched Sienna as she shouted out trivia answers or laughed at dead celebrities while they tried to draw pictures of farm animals. This platonic evening was quickly becoming a favorite memory for him.

A couple hours later, a tiny snore alerted Connor that

she was asleep. As quietly and smoothly as he could muster, he pulled back the blankets to tuck her into bed. She moaned in her sleep, the sound bringing his nether regions back to life. "Down, boy," he chastised himself. It was true that he wanted Sienna, more than he probably wanted anyone before. But Connor felt this was different, because *he* was different. A part of him wanted to stay in her room, to be as close to her as possible, but he wasn't going to push his luck. Karl hadn't discovered them yet, and Connor wanted to keep it that way.

Connor turned off the TV, letting himself out of the room before he could change his mind. As soon as the door clicked shut, he felt he wasn't alone. Turning around, he saw Karl standing outside his door, a well-loved bathrobe cinched at his waist. *Crap.*

"Do I even want to know what's going on there?" Karl's chin jutted toward Sienna's closed bedroom door. Connor felt like a guilty teenager sneaking in after curfew.

Schooling his features, he answered his coach. "Nothing. I just came up to check on Sienna. We talked and watched some TV, and now I'm going to my room."

Karl's arms dropped to his sides, his shoulders deflating with fatigue. "Do I even need to remind you that she is off limits? Never mind either of your reputations, but her mother would skin you alive if she even knew you were *talking* to each other."

Connor bristled at Karl's words. "Sienna's a grown woman. She can hang out with whoever she wants."

The look that crossed Karl's face was sad, defeated. "No, Con, that's where you're wrong. Adult or not, Sienna is more than a daughter. She's an athlete, a brand. She's destined for more greatness before her career is over, and that doesn't involve anything, or anyone, else." Karl looked like he wanted to say more, but he settled for, "Be careful, all right?"

At that moment, Connor didn't feel like a Paralympic hopeful. He felt like the punk he used to be, always chasing the high of a race and the girls. "I don't need to be careful," he bristled.

Stepping forward, Karl slapped Connor's back. "That's where you're wrong. You both need to be careful. When I'm gone for Christmas, I need you to keep your distance."

Connor scoffed, "Karl, we're both adults."

Karl's sigh seemed tired, too tired for someone his age. "I'm going to let you in on a little secret, okay? Sienna's parents think she's here with just me. They would literally freak out and fly back from Italy with flaming torches if they knew the truth. When I came up with the idea to train with both of you, I thought it would help each of you in different ways. It never occurred to me that you'd hit it off and get along. Don't get me wrong, in a way I'm glad. It makes me feel better about leaving for a couple of days."

Something shifted in Connor's gut, and he leaned closer and struggled to keep his voice even. "Do her parents know you're leaving for Christmas?"

Karl looked embarrassed. "Yes, I told her mother this morning."

Connor balled his fists at his sides. He didn't know much about Sienna's family, but he was starting to form a pretty ugly picture. "And they were going to let their daughter spend Christmas alone in an empty ski lodge?"

Karl's head hung low, and he nodded. "Training is all that matters to them. They thought the time alone would keep her focused."

That was all Connor had to hear. "Night, Karl. I'm going to bed." He turned and crossed the hall to his own room, where he fought the urge to slam the door. Sienna deserved a hell of a lot better than she was getting, and it brought his blood to boiling.

Christmas was only two days away, and Connor promised himself he would make it as special as he could for Sienna. In a matter of days, she'd become important to him, and no matter what the future held for them, or their training, he wanted to do something nice. His Golden Girl deserved a golden Christmas.

*

"Are you ignoring me, Sienna?" Karl asked from his perch on the ski lift. He'd insisted on going up to the top with her. No one spoke for a moment, the cold air hanging thick between them. "You're really not speaking to me?"

Sienna pulled her goggles down, careful to slip Karl some side-eye. "I'm speaking to you. I just asked you about my pacing on the final turns." She knew exactly what he meant, but she didn't want to talk about it. Her feelings were hurt. And worse than that, she felt betrayed.

Karl chuckled. "That's not what I meant, and you know it. I feel like a heel for leaving you alone. I'm sorry."

The truth of the matter was, Sienna wouldn't be alone. She'd be with Connor, and for the moment that seemed like enough—plenty. Not that she would let Karl off the hook. "Well, I don't want to talk about it now. Let's talk about my turns."

Sienna noticed Karl's shoulders relax as he shifted back into coach-mode. "All right, let's get to work."

Four hours, several dozen trips down the slopes, and a hot shower later, Sienna was sprawled on her bed with the rest of the bottle of wine from the night before. Connor had left a note on her door saying he'd check in later since he was having a late training with Karl.

She pulled a pillow up to rest her feet and opened a book she'd found in the lodge's library. It was a cheesy, and slightly sleazy, romance novel, and it was just what the doctor ordered. Her fingers eagerly turned the pages as she was transported back to the time of pirates and noble sea captains. While she sipped her wine, her thoughts went back and forth between the leading man in the book and her own leading man. It felt nice to have a leading man, like she had something, someone, just for herself.

The piercing shriek of her cell phone alerted her to an

incoming call from her mother. Sienna sent the call to voicemail. It was empowering not to jump to answer. Granted, she was in her mid-twenties, but she always felt like a child when her mother's face appeared on the screen. Before she could get back to her sea captain, her phone rang again. Apparently, her mother was done with being ignored.

Sienna downed the last of the wine, placed the glass on her nightstand and answered the call. "Hi, Mom," she greeted with the enthusiasm of someone going to the dentist.

"Are you ignoring my calls?" The force behind her mother's voice reverberated off Sienna's eardrum. "Because sending me to voicemail certainly feels like I'm being ignored."

Pinching the bridge of her nose, Sienna stifled a sigh. "I've been busy. You know, with training. Shouldn't you be enjoying Italy?" Her tone had more edge than she usually carried with her mother, but sarcasm wouldn't win her any favors.

"Is this because of Christmas?"

There were a few options Sienna could take. First, she could take the high road and discuss her feelings like the adult she was. Second, she could skirt the issue and go back to their standard conversations based in denial. Not feeling like taking the high road, or even the vague road, Sienna opted for anger instead. And frankly, she reveled in it.

"Of course it's about Christmas. It is my favorite holiday, which I'm pretty sure you and Daddy know. Instead of letting me take a very needed vacation, you ship me off to an isolated training camp. If that wasn't bad enough, now my coach is going home to celebrate with his family. I'll be here with Con—" She cut herself off in the nick of time, not wanting to spill the beans. As much as she wanted to see her family, the notion of her mother flying over to beat Connor with a pair of skis was unappealing. "The point is, I'll be alone for my favorite holiday. So, yeah, I'm pissed off."

Her mother abhorred disrespect, and Sienna would have given good money to see the look on her face. For what felt like an eternity, Sienna listened to the silence on the other line. After a moment, her mother finally responded. "I realize this is hard for you, Sienna. But I will not be disrespected by my own daughter long distance. You are allowed to be disappointed, but you cannot lose focus. Use the time to train, practice, and clear your head. And for God's sake, don't binge-eat. Karl ensured the staff would leave some pre-approved meals for you."

Sienna looked longingly at the empty wine bottle. She hoped that Connor had another secret stash. Discussing her eating habits with her mother was tedious on a good day, but she didn't have a shred of energy for it now. "I'm going to go. You know, to clear my head. Tell Daddy I love him."

It was time for another first as Sienna hung up on her mother. She turned her phone off, placed it in the nightstand drawer, and pulled herself from bed.

A gentle knock at the door shook Sienna from her thoughts. Without looking to see who it was, she opened the door to Connor. Standing in front of her, he looked better than any pirate or sea captain. He held a bag in front of him, the aroma of cinnamon and vanilla wafted toward her. "Have you eaten?" he asked in greeting.

She stepped back and welcomed him into her room. "No. I'm starving."

"Good, because I have a surprise. I brought our date to you." Connor walked to the side table and opened the paper bag. He pulled out a few paper bundles and laid them on the table. Pointing, he rattled off her options. "I have a cinnamon roll, a chicken salad croissant, a cherry Danish, and a brownie." Turning to face her, he smiled and shrugged out of his coat. "There's a bakery at the bottom of the mountain, and I put in a call for delivery."

The grin he flashed was devilish, and suddenly food was the last thing on Sienna's mind. "I'll take a little of everything," she teased.

Rubbing his hands together, Connor beamed. "Good, because I couldn't decide what I wanted either." While he set up their impromptu picnic, he looked over his shoulder and asked, "How was your day? I saw Karl walking around, so you didn't kill or maim him."

Sienna laughed and pulled two bottled waters from the mini fridge. "I forgave him. We'll figure Christmas out on our own." At first, she feared she overstepped. Perhaps Christmas wasn't a big deal to the Shoemaker clan? Maybe he wanted some time alone? Much to her delight, Connor winked at her.

Connor took one of the proffered water bottles and slid an assortment of baked goods her way. "I'm glad you want to spend the day with me because I have a few ideas." The look on his handsome face didn't give anything away.

"A few ideas?" she asked, sneaking a bite from the sandwich. The croissant melted in her mouth, and she felt like she'd died and gone to carby heaven. "This is delicious." And probably loaded with fat, but calories did not count when she was training this hard. Plus, it was nearly Christmas—anything goes!

Connor took a pull from his water, and she watched the muscles in his throat bob up and down. She'd never thought of necks as being erotic, but he was quickly changing her mind. "I'm not going to say a word. Don't you like surprises on Christmas?"

Sienna nodded because she was excited and a little intrigued. "I don't like surprises. I *love* them." She squirmed in her seat as the possibilities washed over her. Visions of Connor naked in a Santa hat came to mind, but she figured his surprises would be less scandalous.

Raising a hand in a salute, Connor beamed. "Then consider me Captain Surprise."

Covering her mouth, Sienna couldn't stifle the snort that erupted. "That might be the lamest superhero name I've ever heard of." She poked him in the bicep as she laughed.

Connor didn't seem deterred by her teasing. "Then

you're really going to love my alias, Captain Christmas." He waggled his eyebrows and reached out to swipe a crumb from her lips. Her skin tingled from the contact, and suddenly the pastries weren't very exciting.

"I'll allow Captain Christmas. It is lame in its own way."

Popping his last bite of brownie into his mouth, Connor chewed thoughtfully. "I can't believe I'm sitting here taking this type of abuse."

Sienna leaned in, closing the distance between them. Their knees knocked as she reached out and tugged on his collar. "Then we better kiss and make up," she suggested. Not waiting for Connor, she swept her tongue over his bottom lip and felt the rumble of his moan surge through her. If she could get that response from a mere kiss, she could not wait to see what else made Connor tick.

"If I didn't know any better," Connor said in between kisses, "I would think you were trying to distract me so you can finish that cinnamon roll."

Curling her fingers into his hair, Sienna tugged him closer to deepen the kiss. "Can't it be both? Maybe I'm just working up an appetite for round two of dessert."

Connor reached out and pulled Sienna into his lap. The chair they were in made it difficult, but she wrapped her legs around his torso and anchored herself in place. "But you forget one important factor," he said as he peppered kisses down her neck. "Captain Christmas cannot be distracted."

The night before had been perfect. Sienna had never felt so cared for as she was during their game show marathon. But this landed differently. This teasing and kissing were more than a bit of fun; this felt like the beginning of real intimacy.

Much like the night before, Connor was the one to end their make-out session. "Don't give me that look," he carefully warned as he carried her to bed. "I want to do this right, Sienna."

There was weight to his words that hit Sienna right in her solar plexus. "You do?"

His mocking Captain Christmas expression was gone, and the Connor who stood before her was different somehow. He looked eager, yet thoughtful. She couldn't miss the creases by his eyes, or the way his jaw tensed as he looked down at her sprawled on the bed.

"You're special, and tomorrow is going to be your best Christmas yet."

Sienna blinked at Connor as her brain did a mental inventory of twenty-five Christmases. Of course she had good memories with her family, but she had no doubt a holiday spent with Connor would be its own version of amazing. They could sit in an abandoned pool house and she'd still think it was worth it. It would be worth it because it was with him.

Looking ahead to the holiday, Sienna was surprised by how little control she had over their plans. What was more surprising was that she liked not having control with Connor. She rarely handed the reins of her life to anyone, but it felt freeing somehow. Maybe it was because she'd stood up to her mother, or even that she said something to Karl, but Sienna was starting to feel like her own person. And dammit, it felt empowering.

CHAPTER SEVEN

It was shockingly simple planning Christmas for Sienna; Connor was pleased to discover. He took his new role as Captain Christmas very seriously. Once Karl was out of the lodge, Connor met with the chef. "It's going to just be the two of us. I know you guys are going home, so I just need to know where to find a few things in the kitchen," he explained while his gaze trailed around the industrial kitchen. The chef, a petite woman in her fifties, didn't seem convinced her kitchen was in good hands.

Connor would not have been ready for the stare-down with the chef if it wasn't for his chat with his brother. Last night when Connor couldn't sleep, he'd made the asinine decision to call Colby.

"What's up?" Colby answered, sounding wide awake for one in the morning. Connor could practically taste the energy drink that his brother was no doubt chugging. He grimaced at the thought.

Connor propped himself up in bed and laughed. "Shouldn't you be sleeping?"

Colby scoffed. "Says the man who called me. What's going on? How's training?" Connor could hear the tension in Colby's voice. This hadn't been the first late-night phone call Connor had made, but at least it wouldn't be depressing.

During the first year after his accident, Connor would drink and fall into deep bouts of depression. It was more than just a beer with dinner; he'd made drinking his new sport. Connor refused help, refused to even talk to anyone, and built up walls around himself. Colby was the only one that got through. When others had given up, Colby persisted.

After a particularly dark night, Colby had been the one who found Connor his therapist. It had also been Colby who'd taken time away from classes to drive his brother to his appointments. Colby had teased, "You think I'm trusting you to get your ass to therapy?"

For his first therapy session, Connor had spent $150 sitting silently in a white room while a frail woman in a gray dress told him his feelings were normal and his thoughts were justified. She'd droned on about the importance of being true to himself, which felt a little too fluffy at first. Then as his sessions became more interactive, he opened up about the trauma of not only losing his career and livelihood, but also scarring his body beyond recognition. The loss of half his leg was the more obvious injury, but there was scar tissue up and down his frame.

And because Connor was an adult, he'd continued going to therapy, finally opening up when he'd seen his third bill and decided that $150 a week was too much to waste. Then he'd started talking. He talked about the error he made in the blink of an eye. How showing up late to a race had caused him to lose focus, caused him to take a turn too quickly when he wasn't ready. How one moment, one second, of lost control had sent him barreling through the air, his bike hot on his heels. In one instant he'd gone from motocross hotshot to a bleeding pile of flesh. The doctors thought he might have to lose more than half his leg, but he'd pulled through. Colby kept saying it was a miracle, but back then Connor didn't feel lucky.

Forcing himself into the present, Connor rubbed his

eyes and relaxed at the sound of Colby's voice. "Everything is fine. Just couldn't sleep."

"Aren't you supposed to be tired from training?" Colby had sounded incredulous. "And speaking of training, how's your hot training partner?"

Connor could only imagine the crude thoughts that had been running through his brother's brain. "I am tired, smart ass. But I'm also distracted."

Chuckling, Colby wouldn't let it go. "I'm guessing because of Ms. Markum? So, tell me, what's going on?" Pausing only a moment, he quickly added, "There better be a story here. There's no way you'd give up your shot with her."

"Tomorrow is Christmas," Connor had said, as if that was all the explanation Colby needed.

Colby sighed. "Shit. Did you want me to come and visit? I didn't even think of that." Connor had heard guilt in Colby's offer, and it made him feel better and worse at the same time.

Shaking his head, Connor replied, "No. That's the last thing I want. It's going to be just me and Sienna for Christmas."

Colby's guilt evaporated as he burst out laughing. "You dog, I see where this is going. You're asking your brother for tips?"

Connor would have punched his brother if they had been together. "No, smart ass. I just need some tips for tomorrow, for something festive." Images of Sienna and his Captain Christmas conversation had made Connor smile. He loved being playful with Sienna.

"This has nothing to do with sex?" Colby had sounded defeated.

"I need help thinking of something festive, or traditional, for tomorrow. I have a tree, and the food is covered, but what else can I do?"

There was a long silence on the other line. Colby's voice had laced in shock. "You're really into her, aren't you? Like, into her into her. This is more than sex." It had been a statement, not a question.

"I am capable of more than one-night stands. I'm almost offended you didn't know that." Connor realized he *had been* offended. His past made him feel two-dimensional sometimes, and moments like that one brought that feeling to the surface. But he wanted to change things; he wanted to have ties to things, to people. And there was one particular person he had in mind.

Colby laughed again. "Cut the crap. You only just discovered this, too. I can't believe Connor freaking Shoemaker is going to settle down."

Connor had been just as surprised as Colby, but he'd also been filled with hope. It felt so rewarding to have someone else's needs in mind, to think about ways to please a woman outside of the bedroom. Although, Connor would be lying if that wasn't part of it. "So, are you going to give me advice, or what?"

Colby had rattled off a string of lewd suggestions before finally offering something useful. "Bake cookies with her."

It was so simple and yet so intimate. "You crazy bastard. I think that's a great idea."

"I'm due to have one every now and again." Colby snorted, and Connor heard the distinct crack of another energy drink being opened. He could practically taste the chemicals from Colorado.

And that was how Connor got to the lodge's industrial kitchen with the chef. "You're sure you know how to use a gas range?" She asked, eyebrow arched.

Connor waved off her concern. "This isn't my first time in a kitchen. I promise I won't destroy anything. Besides, it's just for cookies."

The chef nodded and seemed slightly placated. "We'll all be back tomorrow afternoon for dinner. Remember, there are cinnamon rolls and two plates in the walk-in. You can heat them in the oven and…"

"Please, go home to your family. I've got this."

She relented and left Connor alone with a stack of baking supplies and the feeling of a kid on Christmas morning. Which only seemed fitting, as he was about to get the greatest gift. Captain Christmas was ready to shine!

*

Sienna woke to a feeling of anticipation. Yes, it was Christmas, but it was also her first day alone with Connor. No training, no Karl, no distractions. Crawling out of bed, she showered and took her time getting ready. Never one to sleep in, she was downstairs before eight o'clock. When she made it to the lobby, she was greeted by the smell of cinnamon and the sight of Connor lounging by the Christmas tree. He was clad in jeans and wearing a wooly sweater that was made for a ski lodge. The smile he flashed her was brighter than the twinkle lights hanging around them. It was the perfect Christmas scene.

"Good morning," she said, unable to hide her own smile.

Connor scooted to the side of the couch and patted the empty cushion. "Merry Christmas," he said, leaning in to place a kiss on her cheek.

"Merry Christmas. You're up early," she observed. Like herself, Connor was showered and dressed, looking ready for anything. There was an unmistakable glint in his eyes, and Sienna felt her pulse rate increase. He was definitely up to something. "What got you up so early, Captain Christmas?"

Beaming, Connor leaned over the arm of the couch and retrieved a tray of fresh cinnamon rolls. "I bribed the staff to get us some food before they left for the holiday. I hope you don't mind more cinnamon rolls." Sienna reached out to take one of the delectable-looking buns, but Connor pulled the tray just out of reach. "Oh no, not yet. We're taking these babies on the road."

Confused, Sienna asked, "On the road?"

Connor stood, balancing the tray in one hand and reached for Sienna with the other. He pulled her up and then draped his arm around her. Even with the heavenly aroma of cinnamon, she couldn't miss the distinctive smell of pine that followed Connor everywhere. Nestling into his side, she savored his closeness. He was as warm and fragrant as a campfire.

Guiding them to the patio doors, Connor motioned toward the balcony. "Well, not on the road, but I thought we'd take in the view with breakfast." When Sienna opened the sliding door, she was greeted to a winter wonderland. The mountains were covered in a fresh dusting of snow, as white and fluffy as powdered sugar on beignets. The green branches of the evergreens peaked out, offering a splash of color in the otherwise pristine tableau.

Usually, the sight of fresh powder had Sienna itching for her skis. But now, standing in the crisp air with a hot man—and an even hotter breakfast—beside her, she was content to enjoy the moment. "This is amazing."

Connor walked past her and disappeared around the bend on the balcony. She followed him and discovered the source of the campfire smell. Situated in the corner with the perfect view were lounge chairs, a roaring fire pit, and a pitcher with two mugs. Connor pulled the lid from the pitcher and poured hot chocolate. "Hope you like cocoa with your view," he said, smiling at the expression on her face.

Yes, Sienna loved Christmas. It was a magical time of year. But this was different, this was better. Small gestures from Connor meant so much more than expensive gifts. There was tenderness and heart here, and she had to swallow back tears of gratitude. Captain Christmas had clearly delivered.

"Thank you, Connor. This is amazing."

Once she was seated with a plate of cinnamon rolls and a mug of cocoa, she felt Connor behind her. Before she knew it, he'd draped her in a warm blanket and eased into the chair with her. She saw he was slow to stretch his legs, and she assumed Karl had run him through the wringer the day before in training.

Sienna nodded toward his legs. "Karl run you ragged yesterday?"

Connor mindlessly rubbed above his prosthesis and groaned. "You could say that. Crazy bastard knew I wasn't going to ski today, so he made me pay it forward."

It wasn't that Sienna didn't get sore from training, but she handled it differently. Everything got compartmentalized in her brain, and she didn't think beyond what was needed to win. Seeing Connor suffer from his training gave her pause. "Are you all right?" she asked, placing her now-empty plate on the patio floor. Reaching out, she rested her hand on his thigh and gave him a reassuring pat.

Connor shrugged and slurped from his mug. "I'll be fine. Even after a couple years of this, my skin still gets tender when I'm working out." He didn't meet her gaze, like he was embarrassed.

"Sometimes I need to soak in ice baths to get everything numb after long days on the slopes. You should try it."

A deep chuckle escaped Connor and he shook his head. "That sounds like torture, but if you swear by it, then I'll give it a shot." He covered her hand with his and squeezed.

For a moment, the pair sat and watched the snow sparkling in the morning sun. It was peaceful and romantic, a scene from a movie. When Sienna first arrived at the lodge, she had no idea what to expect from Connor. He seemed arrogant and brash, like he didn't fit her image of a professional skier. Now, she felt foolish for doubting his abilities and drive. Not to mention, he was one of the sweetest, most thoughtful men she'd ever met. "You impressed me," she said, turning to face him.

"You mean breakfast?" His smile crinkled the skin around his eyes, and Sienna wanted to run her fingers over each line and crease.

"No, I mean with all of this. Training, getting ready for the games. You're more than meets the eye, Mr. Shoemaker."

Connor's features softened. "That means more to me than anything else you could have said. Thank you." Sienna curled her frame around his. Connor's arms held her in place, and he kissed the top of her head. "This is the best Christmas morning I've ever had. Thank you for sharing it with me."

Resting her head on his shoulder, Sienna reveled in his embrace. To think of how different things would be without him. Connor, a man she'd hardly thought about before last week, was quickly becoming important to her. If it wasn't for him, she'd be sitting alone on Christmas feeling as lonely as a discarded coffee cup. Now she felt treasured in a way she couldn't have expected from anymore.

"Thank you for making today so special."

"We're just getting started with our Christmas surprises. I aim high when I'm celebrating the holidays with my Golden Girl."

His Golden Girl. What had started as teasing had turned into a pet name Sienna wanted to hear every day for the rest of her life. When she was with Connor, she felt treasured—valued for more than her time down the slopes.

Now, she held Connor's firm grip as he pulled her toward their next Christmas surprise, which was in the kitchen. Letting go of her hand, Connor spun around and extended his arms. A boyish grin cracked his handsome features, and she found herself lost in his excitement. "Ta-da!" he exclaimed, gesturing to one of the stainless-steel workstations. The counter was crammed end-to-end with bags of flour, sugar, chocolate chips, and a stack of mixing bowls.

Unable to stop her own smile, Sienna asked, "What's all this?" She joined Connor, who spread out some of the ingredients. He was truly in the zone, pulling up his sweater sleeves and showing off his toned forearms. Sienna had never found forearms sexy, but she suddenly couldn't focus on anything else. She could tell Connor had said something, so she forced her eyes up and shook her head. "I'm sorry, what?"

As if reading her mind, Connor winked. "I said, we're baking Christmas cookies."

Sienna covered her mouth with her hand to hide her trembling lips. "We are?" she squeaked.

Connor stepped forward, reaching out to pull her to his chest. Much to Sienna's delight, she felt his heart racing as much as hers. "Christmas traditions are important to you—I get that. This is a tradition in my family, and I wanted to share it with you." Leaning back slightly, he gently pinched her chin and angled her face to meet his gaze.

A lone tear escaped, trailing down her cheek as Sienna melted into a puddle of need and desire. None of the men she'd been with had ever listened and followed through with such thoughtfulness. "You did all this, for me?"

Connor chuckled. "Of course. Sienna, you're worth this and a lot more." He kissed her, sweetly at first, before tilting her head back and deepening the kiss. He tasted like chocolate, and she wanted to devour him right in the kitchen. Baking plans be damned.

"We're never going to make it to cookies," she breathed in between kisses. Needing to feel more of Connor, she arched into him, feeling his growing need through his jeans. Before she knew what he was doing, Connor picked her up and sat her on the counter in front of him. Now at eye level, they broke apart long enough to catch their breath.

Eyes as blue as sapphires glinted back at her. "I want you, Sienna. I don't know if I can wait." His voice was thick and laced with tension. His hands gripped her hips, and she rejoiced in the heat of his fingers as they dug into her skin. If she was this turned on fully clothed, she might combust when she felt him skin to skin.

Without asking permission, she tugged Connor's sweater over his head and pulled him in for another kiss. She bit his bottom lip and he growled, the noise sending goosebumps over her flesh. All at once she was hot and cold. "I'm on the pill," she blurted out as she started unbuttoning Connor's jeans. "And I had a test after my ex." There was a full story there that Sienna would share with Connor in time, but she wasn't going there now.

Her statement seemed to shock him out of his lust-filled stupor, and he froze. "Are you sure about this?" The way his question came out sounded more like *he* needed reassuring.

Bracketing his face in her hands, she slid her thumb over his lips and smiled. "I haven't been surer of anything in a long time. Connor, I want you." His eyes darkened as he took in her words, and she loved the way it made her feel. He wanted her, and she could tell it was for who she was, not the polished brand.

Quietly, Connor stared into her eyes for a moment before saying, "I got tested, too. It was a while ago, but I haven't—" He fought to find his words. "I haven't been with anyone since, and I—" She realized he was embarrassed, as if anything he said should make him less of a man. "Since the accident I haven't—"

Sienna wiggled closer until she reached the edge of the counter. "I trust you," she promised, meaning every letter of the words. If someone would have told her she'd be spending Christmas morning naked with Connor Shoemaker, she would have called them crazy. Now she couldn't think of anywhere else to be. She arched near him and felt the last of his resolve crumble.

Connor's hands slid under her sweater; his fingers rough on her smooth skin. Tentatively, he moved up to her breasts. Through the lace of her bra, he slowly rubbed her nipples until they pebbled, moaning at the sensation of her reaction to his touch. "Sienna, I ..." He stopped moving and bit back a string of profanities. He was coming undone. "It's been a while, and, I'm afraid that I ..."

The tremor in his voice broke her, and she kissed him

hard. Sienna hoped her kiss and all her raging emotions would come through, showing Connor that she wasn't the least bit worried. The moment, the man, it all felt natural. As natural as strapping on her skis and gliding down a mountain. This was how her Christmas morning was supposed to be.

Without needing more encouragement, Connor pulled off her sweater and went to work on unhooking her bra. In seconds, they were both naked and breaking numerous health code violations in the kitchen. For as much as Connor might have been worried about his performance, he needn't be. Sienna was seeing stars before he even entered her. He took his time, paying special attention to what she needed, following the moans and angles of her body.

When they were finished, they lay in each other's arms on the kitchen floor on a pile of their discarded clothes, warmed by the nearby oven and their own racing pulses. Connor held her tightly against his frame, whispering in her ear about how incredible she was. "That was everything," he mused, nibbling the skin behind her ear. Sienna wriggled against him, and he laughed. "If you keep this up, we'll never make it to cookies."

"This truly might be the best Christmas ever," she said, unable to hold back her growing grin.

And it was. It was more than Connor and his Captain Christmas routine—it was how weightless and happy she felt. This was more than a sugar rush or the high that comes from earth-shattering sex. No, this was more. Sienna felt like a woman, plain and simple. Not someone with a strict training schedule, not someone with years of expectations pushing down on her shoulders. Christmas felt like the beginning of something big, and it had nothing to do with the slopes. Perhaps it was too soon to feel this way, but Sienna felt she was falling in love.

CHAPTER EIGHT

As the sun set and the lodge settled into the quiet that only night can bring, Connor brought out another surprise. "Hope you're hungry for something beyond sugar and sugar," he teased, savoring the look of utter contentment on Sienna's lovely face. Her gray eyes looked tired, but in the sappy way that came from a day of enjoyment.

She sat curled up on the couch, her face illuminated by the lights of the Christmas tree. Connor felt his breath hitch as she watched him approach with their dinner. He could get used to seeing that face every day. It was pointless to tell himself he wasn't in deep with Sienna. He had never felt this way about a woman. Ever.

"Don't keep me in suspense. What does Captain Christmas have planned for dinner?"

Not only had Connor never had a jumble of feelings for someone, but he'd also never had cutesy nicknames with previous girlfriends. It never seemed like something he wanted in his life, but now he craved hearing the moniker.

Sienna clapped her hands and kicked out her legs on the couch. Connor insisted they eat their dinner by the tree, and she was not upset about his plan.

"Pasta," he said as he handed her a bowl. The heavenly

73

aroma of cheese and garlic filled the air between them, and Connor exhaled a sigh of relief when he saw Sienna's already happy expression morph into unbridled bliss.

"Really?" She gasped as she took her bowl and hugged it to her chest. "How did you know I asked Santa for carbs on top of carbs for Christmas?"

Once Connor was seated next to her, Sienna took a bite of pasta and swooned.

"I'm glad you approve," he said, unable to stop the smile from taking over his face. If he thought competitor Sienna was hot, she had nothing on playful Sienna.

Briefly putting her fork down, she closed the distance between them and kissed his cheek. "Thank you," she whispered. "This has been the best Christmas ever." She let her words sink in before adding, "I mean it."

Connor harumphed. "You're telling me you wouldn't rather be in Italy eating the real deal?"

Sienna rested her hand on his leg and squeezed; the pressure gentle but sincere. "This is the real deal, Connor."

He knew she meant more than the pasta, but he wasn't quite sure how to respond.

Not that he was complaining, but Connor wasn't used to dating women who wanted to share more than a night of passion. No one had ever looked at him this way—even before he lost his leg.

Through the growing lump in his throat, Connor said, "Thank you for spending your Christmas with me."

"My pleasure." Sienna kissed him again, this time on the lips and with so much gusto she almost knocked over her bowl.

Pulling back, Connor tucked a lock of dark hair behind her ear. "It will be, once we get our energy back." He waggled his eyebrows and Sienna snorted.

"You are relentless. Good thing we're both athletes." She picked up her dinner and ate the rest of her meal in three bites. Patting her flat belly, she groaned. "Actually, we'll need at least another round so I can burn off all this food."

Raising an eyebrow, Connor couldn't stop the words that spewed from his mouth. "You know you're stunning, right? Like blindingly gorgeous. When I told my brother I met you, he literally squealed. He's a grown-ass man, and he fangirled. You're every guy's fantasy, Sienna."

With a dramatic eye roll, Sienna looked away. Her gray gaze slid to the Christmas tree, her attention focused on a cluster of red ornaments. "It's really hard sometimes to keep that façade going," she said, so quietly Connor thought he hadn't heard her.

"What do you mean?" His meal forgotten; Connor tugged her closer until she was in his lap. He rested his chin on the top of her head and waited for her to continue.

"I'm a brand, not a woman. I need to be polished and perfect. Thin, but not too thin that I lose muscle. It is absolutely exhausting to keep it all going, but I don't know any other way."

Connor thought back to when they first met, and he was surprised to realize he hadn't noticed how tired she was. She looked like the Sienna Markum the public knew, not this relaxed woman he held in his arms. "I had no idea things were so hard for you. I'm sorry."

Sienna shrugged. "I know I'm lucky, but lately I've wondered what else is out there for me." Connor felt a kick in his ribcage at the mention of her future, and he secretly hoped that he would fit somewhere. He didn't know how it would work, but he couldn't imagine not being with his Golden Girl.

"What else would you like to do?"

A chuckle bubbled up from Sienna. "Not. A. Clue. I just know I want to make my own decisions. I'm tired of being under everyone's control."

Connor assumed she meant her parents, but he wasn't going to pry. She was already opening up more than he expected.

For a few moments they were quiet, leaning into each

other and enjoying the moment. The only sound in the room was the ticking of the clock on the wall. Just as Connor thought Sienna had fallen asleep, she asked, "What about you? What do you want to do after the games?"

"I don't know." His admission was out of his mouth before Connor could second guess himself. "I guess I'm trying to prove myself, and I hope I'll be polishing a medal."

Sienna pulled her head back so their gazes locked. "You don't need to prove yourself, Connor. You have overcome so much in the last few years. You should be proud of everything you've accomplished."

Tears threatened and Connor blinked frantically. No one, other than Colby, had said they were proud of him since his accident. He had heard everything else from people—pity, ridicule, discomfort, but never pride.

"Thanks," he said, his voice barely audible.

Sienna reached out and cupped his cheek, tracing the line of scruff before continuing her argument. "I can tell this makes you uncomfortable, but you need to know you're doing amazing things. Truly."

"Yeah, I think Captain Christmas is ready for more sex," Connor joked, but his attempts at humor were thwarted when Sienna shook her head.

"We can certainly have more sex," she said with a smirk, "but I'm not finished praising you."

Unable to handle the well of emotions threatening to burst through his tear ducts, Connor tickled Sienna's side and waited for her to laugh. "You were saying?" he asked in between tickles. She yelped as his hand slid under her sweater and he found the soft skin of her stomach. He was delighted to discover that the constellation of freckles on her shoulder made it all the way down to her hips. He felt like Galileo charting out the swoops and swirls on her skin.

"Okay, you win!" Sienna shrieked as she pulled herself free of his grasp. "You're a horrible person, and this is the worse day of my life."

Connor leaned back on the couch, satisfied his emotions

could play hide and seek a while longer. "Thank you. That is the honesty I need in my life."

Sienna reached out and took Connor's hand, pulling him to his feet. Their prosthesis clattered together as she yanked him closer for a kiss. "Let's take this party upstairs." Without hesitation, he followed her to her bedroom. As they walked hand in hand, Connor realized he was ready to follow Sienna anywhere. Even if she did want to talk about feelings and poke at the sore spots he'd kept covered since his accident, Connor knew he would slice himself open if it meant being with Sienna. If this was what grown-up relationships were like, he was done playing Peter Pan.

*

While Sienna had every intention of tearing Connor's clothes off, she had other plans for the immediate future. As soon as the door clicked shut, Connor scooped her up into his arms and playfully tossed her onto the bed.

She giggled, a sound she hadn't made in far too long, and watched Connor pull his sweater off over his head. During the last several hours she became intimately acquainted with the fine specimen that was Connor Shoemaker. His legs were toned and hard as rocks, the cords dipping and rising like the turns of her favorite slopes. And then there was his six-pack. Sienna found herself looking for nickels to hide between the rows of muscle—her fascination with his body was becoming a problem.

"As much as I like the view," she said, licking her lips in appreciation, "I thought we could watch a movie first." Connor didn't hesitate, reaching for his sweater to get redressed. "Hey now," she teased, "I don't mean we have to watch the movie fully clothed."

Raising an eyebrow, Connor asked, "What movie?"

Sienna clasped her hands in front of her and offered a sheepish expression. "*Rudolph*?"

Connor threw his head back and laughed, a deep sound

that echoed off the walls of her bedroom. "Yeah, I can't be half-naked during a children's movie."

"It's a Christmas movie," Sienna helpfully amended. "And, besides, I'm not done objectifying you." She wasn't sure, but Connor seemed to flinch at her words. "What's the matter?"

Connor shrugged, his blue eyes not quite meeting hers. "Guess I'm more of a Frosty guy."

Sienna gestured around her before patting the top of the bed. "This is a safe space, remember? Now sit down and talk to me." She arched an eyebrow. "I'm guessing that look is based on more than our taste in holiday movies."

Connor hesitated, still standing a few feet from the bed. He looked anywhere but at her, and Sienna felt a growing sense of dread. Had she pushed things too far today? Was Connor just a nice guy and she misinterpreted his kindness for actual feelings?

"I think I'm going to grab something from my room," Connor said over his shoulder as he stalked toward the door. His shoulders were bunched up by his ears, the tension radiating off him in waves.

"Wait!" Sienna hated the feeling of desperation that surged through her, but she'd be damned if she let Connor run away. She caught up to him in the hallway and snatched his wrist, stopping him before he could open his door. "Connor, please talk to me. I'm sorry if I upset you. It's just that—" But her excuses died on her tongue when he finally turned around.

Connor's eyes shone in the fluorescent lighting, and the sight nearly broke her heart. "You have done nothing wrong," he said, his voice low and rough.

"Then why are you running away?"

Connor threw his arms in the air, the gesture brimming with frustration. "Because I don't know what I'm doing." Sienna held her tongue, knowing the slightest distraction could stop Connor's explanation cold. "You're amazing, Sienna. You're confident, gorgeous, funny, and so silly I can't stand it." Finally, a hint of a smile threatened his lips, but Sienna didn't relax. There was more here, and she didn't think it was all good.

"I'm broken," Connor said, his shoulders slumping at the admission. "I haven't felt like myself in three years, since the accident."

Despite her best efforts to keep her mouth shut, Sienna interrupted. "You are not broken. You're a world-class athlete."

"Who lost his leg and hasn't been able to sleep through the night in years. Sienna, I'm worried I'm going to taint you. That my baggage will weigh you down." He balled his fist and pounded his chest. "I don't want to pull you down."

Sienna's lip trembled as his words hit her. "You won't. You're wrong."

"I'm not, I'm—"

Letting her arms drop to her sides, Sienna continued her argument. "You're wrong," she said with more conviction. "You are dedicated to your training. You're a good brother, and I can tell you care about Karl. What you've done for me today alone makes you a candidate for sainthood, and you're a hell of a skier. I know you lost a lot in the accident. Having been born without my leg, I don't understand that feeling of loss. But what I do know is that you're a competitor, Connor. You're here to compete, and you're here to win. I don't see a broken man; I see a strong one."

Connor shook his head, his eyes brimming with tears. "You don't have to say that."

Sienna stepped closer, reaching out squeeze his shoulder. "You're right, I don't. But I'm going to keep saying it until you listen." She pulled his face closer and kissed him softly. The passion from a moment ago was gone, in its place was more heart and tenderness.

Tugging her close, Connor rested his head on her shoulder and shook with sobs. "You're the first woman to make me feel like myself," he said in between gasps. "Sienna, you don't realize what that means."

Oh, yeah, she did, because she was feeling the same way. She was a goner. There was no point denying she was in love with Connor. Between his honesty and the passion burning between them, she'd never felt this way before. It was exciting and terrifying in equal measure. The one thing that didn't scare Sienna, though, was the future, because she had a feeling this was the beginning of her next chapter. Yes, she was still going for the gold, but this time she had more than a training partner by her side. She thought she'd found a life partner, too.

CHAPTER NINE

Connor couldn't think of the last time he was this happy—or this conflicted. On one hand, he was buoyant as he walked down to the lobby the next morning. He'd woken up with Sienna wrapped around him like a koala bear on a eucalyptus tree. Her dark hair fanned over the pillow, and he couldn't stop himself from sneaking a sniff of her citrusy locks. *Yeah, he was a goner.*

Karl was due back any minute, but Connor wouldn't let the return to normal dull his spirits. He had his own demons to take care of that. What happened yesterday was more than just amazing sex and Christmas cookies. Last night was a form of intimacy he never shared with a woman before. He told Sienna things—his most buried secrets and fears—and she hadn't balked or ran away. No, his Golden Girl continued to surprise him. She stood firm, not letting him run away from his feelings, or from her.

In the wee hours of the morning, Connor thought about the current state of his life. When he'd stopped bed-hopping, it never occurred to him to want more from a woman, from a partner. The more time he'd spent with Sienna, the more certain he was that she belonged by his side. It scared the hell out of him, and he was eternally grateful that she was stronger than him—that she seemed to want this as much as he did.

Once he'd followed her back to her room, they'd settled in for a Christmas movie marathon. For as long as he'll live, Connor will never forget how Sienna's gray eyes danced when Rudolph got called in to save Christmas. As the credits rolled, she clapped like she'd just witnessed a Tony-award-winning Broadway play. Yet for his teasing, her holiday enthusiasm was contagious and made Connor feel like the world was a better place because she was in it.

After a morning of cuddling and sharing the last cinnamon roll, Sienna had gone off to get ready for Karl's return. Connor went to the gym and tried to work off some of his restless energy, but he knew it was no use. It would take more than an hour on the treadmill to calm his nerves. He knew he did the right thing opening up to Sienna, but he couldn't escape the raw feeling that crept over his skin. He just had to trust her when she said she wasn't going anywhere.

Connor showered and stalked downstairs to find Sienna. If they were lucky, they'd have another few hours before Karl's return and the training began. Connor wanted to soak up every moment with her before they had to go back to training. Although on this gorgeous morning, training was the last thing on his mind. When he got downstairs, he saw Sienna on the balcony. Leaning over the railing, she seemed a million miles away. He eased the door open but did not step closer. He was too captivated by the scene in front of him.

"If you're going to stand out here, it better be with your arms around me," she said over her shoulder. Her dark hair cascaded down her back, the perfect contrast to the snow-covered peaks in the distance.

Letting the door close behind him, Connor paced to Sienna and did as she requested. They fit perfectly together, his chin resting on her shoulder. "Good morning," he said between kisses down her neck. Her skin was as soft as rose petals.

"Mmm, good morning." Sienna leaned back into Connor, a sigh escaping her lips. "You better behave. Otherwise we'll give Karl quite the show." For all her faux complaining, she did nothing to slow down their make-out session, curling her fingers into his shoulders as she pulled him closer still.

The mention of Karl's return shook Connor back to the moment. When he was in the gym, he tried to figure out their next move. No doubt Karl would be disappointed in him for crossing a line, but Connor wasn't worried about his coach's feelings right now. No, he was worried about his Golden Girl.

"Do you think we should tell Karl?" As soon as he put voice to the question, Connor felt his skin prickle with nerves.

Sienna snorted. "No."

Connor shook his head, a little confused by her response. "You don't think we should be honest?" A feeling of unease crept up his spine. Was Sienna ashamed to be with him?

Tilting her head to the side, Sienna was quiet a moment. She caught Connor's gaze and blinked. "Oh crap, Connor. This has nothing to do with you. I wouldn't want to tell Karl about anything in my personal life."

Incredulous, he asked, "You don't trust Karl?"

"I do trust him, but I know he'd tell my parents." There was obviously a lot he still didn't understand about her relationship with her parents, but Connor knew they didn't have enough time to delve into that complication now.

Nevertheless, her admission felt like a slap on the face. "And that's a problem?"

Sienna pulled back, a frown marring her lovely features. "Yes, it's a problem. Until the games are over, my life isn't my own." She let out an exhale, and Connor felt her pulling away inch by inch. "This," she said gesturing between them, "is important to me. I'm not going anywhere; I mean that. I just need to tell them my own way."

Connor frowned, but he didn't want to start an argument. After everything they did and said over Christmas, he knew Sienna wouldn't let him down. She was all things good, and he knew he was lucky to have her in his life.

Trailing his hands up her arms to her shoulders, he leaned in and gently pecked her cheek. "Then I guess I'll keep my big mouth shut."

Sienna smiled, her body deflated in relief at their agreement. "Just for now."

There was a lot left unsaid, but Connor saw a car approaching the lodge. "Looks like we'll have to put a pin in this discussion. Here comes Karl."

Suddenly Connor felt hopeless, like everything from their Christmas together was going to crumble down the mountain like an avalanche. "I wish we had more time, just the two of us."

Putting his fears to rest, Sienna turned and pulled him to her lips for one more kiss. It held a sense of urgency, but he savored the feel of her lips on his. "When this is all over, the training, the games"—she paused and let out a long, slow breath—"I want us to make this work. Connor, I think I—" Her words were cut off by the blaring cell phone in her pocket. Sienna mumbled and pulled it from her jacket. Giving it a glance, she rejected the call and shoved her phone away.

Connor saw the tension in her face and figured it was her mother calling. Even though she didn't talk a lot about her mother, Sienna had made it clear their relationship was complicated. "Do you need to take that?"

Sienna shook her head and reached out for his hands. "No, it's just my mother." Pulling Connor to her, they started kissing, as if they were not about to get an audience. Their time together was so precious, and he greedily took everything she offered him. He cataloged every freckle on her face, every curve of her frame—he wanted to look back on every second of their Christmas together.

Now it was Connor's phone that started to buzz. He reluctantly pulled back and shook his head. "I'm sorry—it might be Colby." In all the excitement of Christmas, he'd neglected his brother. But Connor knew one thing for certain—Colby always broke the bro code for a gorgeous woman. He smiled then, a secret smile, as he anticipated telling Colby about Sienna and him. Although his brother would be disappointed that the talk would center around cookies instead of more adult activities. Somethings just didn't need to be shared between brothers.

But it wasn't Colby, it was a text from Karl. All it said was, *I'm sorry.* Connor didn't know what it meant, but it made his hackles rise.

Sienna leaned over to see his screen. "Is it bad news?" He felt her stiffen beside him, as if sensing a shift in their orbit.

"I would say so," a woman's voice echoed behind them. Connor didn't even need to ask who she was, because the ashen look on Sienna's face left no room for confusion. Scrooge looked more excited to see the Ghost of Christmas Future.

"Mom, what are you doing here?" Sienna croaked, letting her arms fall to her sides as she stepped away from Connor.

A knot formed in Connor's stomach as Sienna widened the space between them. The confident woman he'd seen over the last few days had shifted into someone he barely recognized. Her shoulders drooped and her eyes creased with tension.

"I think the more important question is what are *you* doing here?" Sienna's mother asked as she stepped forward and assessed Connor. Her eyes took their time, starting at his tousled hair and sliding down to his prothesis. Her face was unreadable, which only heightened his anxiety. "You must be Connor," she surmised.

Connor stepped forward and extended his hand. While

he didn't have a lot of practice meeting the mothers of the women he dated, he was raised with enough manners to fake it. "Yes, ma'am, Connor Shoemaker."

Sienna's mother's arms stayed cemented in place, and she stepped around to her daughter. It was a rudely dismissive gesture, and Connor did not like it one bit. He wasn't used to high society snobs, and his fists balled at his sides.

Needing something more productive to do, Connor trained his eyes on Sienna. He could see her taking in their exchange, and he hoped she was half as appalled as he was. Before he could say anything, Karl joined them on the balcony with a man in his late fifties. Karl was panting like he'd just run a mile. The other man looked concerned but not angry.

"Daddy!" Sienna exclaimed as she ran to her father. While her mother was intimidating, her father appeared laid back and pleasant.

Closing the distance between him and his daughter, he pulled her into a hug and practically lifted her off the ground. "Sweetheart, it's good to see you."

Their reunion was cut short when Sienna's mother stepped next to them. "We can continue this in the car. David, go get Sienna's bags. Sienna, make sure you have your gear. Our flight leaves in less than two hours."

Connor couldn't believe what he was hearing, and judging from Karl's expression, he wasn't alone. "Beverly, I've been trying to tell you, Sienna's training cannot take a hit like this."

That was clearly the wrong thing to say. Beverly whipped around and stalked toward Karl, who practically shrunk to half his size. "No, Karl. I don't think *you* understand. I sent my daughter, my champion, to train to win the gold. What I get instead is a total lack of respect for my time and money." Waving a hand in Connor's direction, she spat, "And to make it worse, I wasn't even paying for private lessons. I was paying for my daughter to be assaulted by this ruffian!'"

Connor had heard enough. "Wait a minute," he growled, stepping toward Sienna. It was one thing for her mother to look down her nose at him, but allegations like this were a different story. "Nothing like that happened here."

To his credit, her father stepped forward and took Connor's side, if only for a moment. "I think we all just need to take a deep breath. I don't believe anything untoward happened here." Turning to his daughter, he confirmed, "Isn't that right, Sweetheart?"

Finally, some of the fire came back to Sienna. Her back stiffened and her shoulders squared. "Mom, this is ridiculous. You have no idea what you are talking about."

Just as Sienna was finding her words, Beverly cut them off with a wave of her hand. "I'm done here; we're all done here." She hiked her purse high on her shoulder and pointed at her husband. "Get her bags, now." Turning back to Sienna, her eyes ablaze, she ordered through clenched teeth, "Get your gear."

Connor stepped closer to Sienna, but Karl reached out and took his sleeve. "It's not worth it," he whispered. But Connor couldn't disagree more. In less than ten minutes everything he thought he'd found with Sienna was being ripped from him, and there had to be something he could do. He hadn't felt this hopeless since the accident.

Beverly walked up to Connor and looked him in the eye for the first time. "Stay right where you are, Mr. Shoemaker. This is not your battle."

Connor shook off Karl's grasp. "The hell it isn't. Sienna and I ..."

Smirking, Beverly straightened to her full height and poked Connor in the chest with her manicured finger. "There is no 'Sienna and I,' do you understand me? Stay away from my daughter. She has come too far to have someone like you interfere in her dreams."

The words stung, cutting Connor right down to the bone. Certainly, he had felt less-than over the years, but never as much as he did in that moment. He looked toward Sienna, hoping she would stand up for what they had, what they could have. Much to his distress, he only saw Sienna's back as she was led into the lodge.

Feeling the world crumbling beneath him, Connor stepped back and fell into a lounge chair. Now he felt raw, exposed for the failure he was. Karl placed a hand on his shoulder. "I'm sorry, Con." Shaking off his coach's support, Connor got up and turned for the door. "Don't go after her. Give her some time."

Connor bristled and shook his head. "I'm getting my gear. Time to hit the slopes."

He couldn't stay on the balcony another second. Just as when he was recovering from his accident, Connor needed speed to get him back to himself. Sitting around moping wasn't going to do him any favors. From her inaction, Sienna had made her choice. Connor could not agree with it, but he'd be damned if he got in her way. His Golden Girl deserved the best, even if it wasn't him.

CHAPTER TEN

Sitting in the back of the rental car, wedged between her suitcase and her duffle bag, Sienna felt five years old. Over the last thirty minutes she had been humiliated, reprimanded, and scolded to within an inch of her life. She slunk back in her seat and watched the gorgeous Aspen scenery whip past the window. None of this felt like real life.

In the haste to get her parents away from Connor, Sienna had accidentally cut herself off from him as well. She wanted to tell him how sorry she was, how she was going to make it right, but she didn't have the opportunity or the words.

"So, what now?" she asked the back of her parents' heads. They hadn't looked at her since they ushered her into the car. "I go back home and wait for the Paralympics? I'm done with training?"

Beverly huffed. "Enough with the sarcasm, Sienna. It never looks good on you. You're going back with Vlad. He's unavailable until the New Year, but that will give you the precious vacation you've been whining about."

Feeling a fresh wave of anxiety crash over her, Sienna had to focus on breathing. Vlad was her former coach, and an absolute tyrant. Unlike her time with Karl, which was spent with conversation and planning, Vlad would shout and throw things and act like any misstep was failure. The big difference with Karl was that her errors were seen as learning opportunities. Karl never raised his voice or made her feel nervous—or God forbid useless.

Thinking ahead to her last days before Vlad was back in her life, Sienna knew this wasn't a vacation. Her mother would be her shadow. Sienna wanted to rebel, revolt and shout about how unfair it all was. About how much she'd enjoyed having Karl as a coach. About how much she didn't want to compete anymore if it meant missing out on things like laughter and love.

Sienna felt hollow, completely gutted, like a fish gone to market. She'd only known Connor for a couple weeks, but he'd changed her. It was magical to be more than an athlete, more than competition. Sienna felt like herself, but also desirable. What Connor had done for her, what he had given of himself, was so special. And when the chips were down, she'd been a coward and run away. Abandoned him when he needed her the most.

How would he ever believe that she was in love with him? How could she have been so reckless with his heart? With her own heart?

Sienna patted around her pockets for her cell phone, eager to reach out to Connor. She texted him. *I'm so sorry, about all of this. can I call you tonight?* He didn't respond immediately, and she didn't blame him. It did not stop her from filling his inbox with messages of how she missed him and how horrible she felt leaving the way she did. He had every right to be angry, she just hoped he'd find a way to forgive her.

*

Not only did Connor not respond immediately, he didn't respond at all. Sienna peppered his phone with texts and voicemails for weeks, each filled with apologies and pleas for forgiveness. Her heart was broken, and she could only assume Connor's was as well. His silence spoke more than words ever could. She had to respect his need to move on, even if it killed her.

A month flew by with training, diets and gym routines as the games approached. Working with Vlad took all the joy from training. His harsh words cut her down every time she strapped on her skis. "Head up," he'd shout from his perch at the top of the hill. "Are you deaf or just stupid?"

At first, Sienna had a million retorts on the tip of her tongue. She'd wanted to tell that vodka-drinking bastard to go back to Russia and leave her in peace. But over her dinners of poached salmon and steamed broccoli, her mother had continued to wear her down. "That's quite enough lemon. Too much acid in your food can make you look older. We need you fresh-faced for the games. Don't forget about your sponsorships. They want a young, nubile woman."

"That's funny," Sienna said on a huff, "I thought they wanted a gold-medal winning athlete." She stormed away from the table—her appetite forgotten—her dog Roscoe following her out of the dining room. The sweet pup had become her only friend, a fact that depressed Sienna more than anything.

Sienna didn't even see herself when she looked in the mirror. There were no laughter lines, no sparkle in her eyes. All that remained inside her was the desire to win. Sienna promised herself that when she won the gold, she would walk away from all of it as a champion. If she was giving up a normal life, she wanted it to be worth something. Finally, it was time to make her own way in the world.

For all the drama during her recent training, it didn't stop Sienna from thinking of Connor. She'd stopped trying to reach out, even though he was never far from her mind. Through a few texts with Karl she'd learned that Connor remained at the lodge to train until right before the games. Her former coach had ensured Sienna that Connor was fine, but she didn't relax at his reassurances. If anything, she wouldn't believe anyone until she saw the man herself.

Finally after weeks of harsh training sessions and fights with her mother, it was time for Sienna to leave for the games. On the morning she left for the airport, she wasn't thinking about the competition or what she needed to do to prepare. What she thought about was seeing Connor again. She'd taken to watching interviews of him before bedtime. Granted it wasn't the same as having the man with her in bed, but at least she could fall asleep to the sound of the soothing timbre of his voice. It wasn't much, but it was all she had.

The days before the Paralympics was press time. Interviews for TV, vlogs, social media, and magazines filled competitors' time. The upside of the media circus was Sienna would finally see Connor. While he wasn't responding to her texts, Karl was. At the first night of media interviews, Sienna found Karl in the hallway of the convention center. Clad in another thick sweater, his hair seemed to be a shade lighter. Whether it was the stress of the games or the stress of the holidays, she wasn't certain.

"Karl!" she screamed from across the crowd.

Sienna was one of the biggest draws in the games, and she usually tried to stay under the radar. Dozens of people's gazes followed her as she ran to Karl. There was no grace in her movements as she pushed through the crowd. They hugged briefly before Sienna started looking of Connor.

Sensing her question, Karl answered, "He's still in his room."

Sienna couldn't help it, she felt her eyes misting over. Granted she didn't expect a Hollywood-style reunion at the press junket, but she wanted more than this.

"Oh," was all she could say.

Rubbing the back of his neck, Karl struggled to find the right words. "His interviews are tomorrow. In the meantime, he's laying low."

Like a parrot, Sienna repeated herself lamely. "Oh."

Karl sighed. "He's going to kill me for telling you this, but he's in room 1876. Give him a break, okay?"

There were three interviews scheduled for Sienna that evening, but she couldn't care less. Her thoughts all pointed to a certain competitor with blue eyes and a crooked smile. She was going to make this right.

"Thank you, Karl."

He shrugged. "I'm sorry about how all of this ended up." He sounded tired, and Sienna appreciated his candor.

Sienna shook off his apology. "I'm the one who should apologize. For my mother, for dropping you, for everything. You deserved better as a coach, but also as my friend."

Karl gave her a brief hug before stepping back. "Apology accepted but not needed. Thanks, Sienna." He glanced over her shoulder and grimaced. "I better head out. I'll be watching and cheering for you. Remember your corners and your speed." He waggled a finger at her and winked. "This is your games, Sienna. You've got this."

She cupped his shoulder and fought a fresh round of tears. Karl's faith in her meant more than he could know. She was used to the pressure, but she wasn't used to a coach's faith and support. "Thank you. I won't let you down." What Karl couldn't possibly understand was that she meant more than the gold medal. She had her sights set on the big picture.

Before Sienna could leave in search for Connor, her mother took her hand and pulled her toward one of the interview rooms. Clearly Karl had seen her first, and she couldn't blame the man for turning tail and running. Feeling helpless, Sienna trudged on. Her heart screamed for her to make a grand gesture, to get to Connor and show him that she meant what she said, to tell him that he's the most important person in her life. But it felt hollow. He deserved more.

As they approached the interview room, Sienna spotted a ghost. Her steps faltered and her pulse jumped. The man could be Connor's twin, with wavy, sandy hair and a boyish grin. Currently he stood chatting up a young woman who worked for one of the networks. The look she gave him showed she was just as interested.

After the young woman said something, he threw his head back in laughter. The sound was so familiar, Sienna felt her heart rattling in her rib cage. This had to be Colby.

Just as they got closer to Colby, he waved at the woman and turned in the opposite direction. "Wait." Sienna gasped, coming to an abrupt stop.

Not understanding the issue, Beverly rolled her eyes. "Sienna, NBC is waiting. You've done these interviews for years, don't get precious now."

Sienna didn't want her mother to know who that man was, so she came up with a plan. "Meet me there? I need to go to the ladies' room."

Her mother wasn't buying it. "Your makeup is flawless."

Reaching up, Sienna patted her cheeks and frowned. She needed a better plan. "Well, um." She looked around and saw Colby's retreating form. "You can make sure the lighting is ready." Her mother was a stickler with lighting, so Sienna knew this tactic would work.

"Good point. That hack at Fox made you look like a ghost." With a curt nod, her mother turned and headed toward the interview room.

Now that her mother was safely out of earshot, Sienna sprinted toward Colby. She had no plan, no idea what to say, but she knew he could help her. "Colby?" she asked as she tapped his shoulder. Fortunately the young woman he was flirting with had already left. Sienna didn't want this to be more complicated than it had to be.

Colby spun around, and his grin was so bright it lit up the venue. "Golden Girl," he mused. Sienna was shocked when he pulled her in for a bear hug, pushing the air out of her lungs. "It's nice to finally meet you."

"It is?" Sienna asked dubiously.

Colby chuckled. "It is if you're here to win back my brother."

Sienna let out a breath and almost hugged him again. "I need your help. How does your brother feel about grand gestures?"

Colby lifted an eyebrow, but when Sienna explained her sudden plan, he was smiling even broader. "If you even do half of that, he'll be putty in your hands."

"You think so? It's not too late?" Sienna's hands were clasped in front of her in prayer, realizing for the first time how much she needed this to work. It was her last chance at winning back the man she loved.

With a shrug, Colby looked a little uncomfortable. "I'm not going to stand here and talk about feelings"—he shuddered—"but my brother has been a lovesick fool ever since Christmas."

Despite the jolt of excitement at Colby's declaration, Sienna was still skeptical. "Then why hasn't he returned any of my calls or messages? I've been trying to get a hold of him for weeks."

Colby lifted a shoulder and sighed. "He just doesn't want to get in the way of your dreams."

Sienna shook her head. "The trouble with that theory is that Connor is my dream."

CHAPTER ELEVEN

When Connor had been in motocross, nothing got in his head before a competition. No matter the size of the venue, he would get in the zone and stay there until his bike had been put away, he was covered in dirt, and his body ached from the effort. In stark, and unfortunate, contrast, here he was at the Paralympics, and all he could do was think about Sienna.

Sienna, who ran away with his heart. Sienna, who was in this hotel preparing for her own competition. The final race that would prove all her years of focus and drive were worth it. He knew his girl, and she would get her gold and prove to the world that she was the champion they deserved.

Rubbing at his chest, his heart ached with the need to see her. But Connor promised himself he was not going to get in her way. She was so close, and he'd be damned if he was the reason she fell short of her goals. If they were truly meant to be, they would find a way when their skis were put away and the gold was around her neck.

Easing back on his bed, he read through the interview schedule of his fellow competitors. Connor wasn't a fool, and he knew that Sienna's interviews were scheduled to air the hour before her race.

Just then, Colby barged into his room and plopped down on the bed. "What's up? Ready to grab some dinner?"

"Why did I give you a key to my room?"

"You didn't," Colby said with a chuckle. "But I have my ways of being very persuasive with that hottie at the front desk." His brother made a lewd gesture and Connor threw a pillow at him.

"Real nice, man."

Connor took a moment to study his brother. Something didn't seem right in that moment. Now, Colby was a poker player and could spin a yarn to capture anyone's attention. Yet his brother was a terrible secret keeper. His jaw was just a little too tight, his eyes a little too pinched. He was hiding something.

"What's gotten into you?" Connor asked, raising an eyebrow.

Colby shrugged and pushed his brother to the side of the massive bed. "Scoot over, you're hogging the bed."

"You mean, my bed? Feel free to go next door and crash in your room, which I also paid for."

Flipping his big brother the bird, Colby picked up the remote and turned to the network airing the interviews. "Real nice, dude. You're going to throw your own brother into the street?"

"I was thinking I'd throw you out to your well-appointed suite, but however you want to spin this."

Once more, Colby offered his brother a rude gesture and stayed firmly planted on the bed. "Shut up. I want to watch the interviews before tonight's competition." Still, his brother could not meet his gaze.

Connor tensed, not wanting to watch the interviews, let alone with Colby present. Faking the worst yawn in history, he covered his mouth and sighed. "Why don't you head out? I might grab a nap."

"Nope, we're gonna watch this." Colby tucked the remote under his leg and leaned back contentedly, looking like the cat that caught the canary.

Connor wasn't fooled. "What are you up to?"

Colby pulled his fingers over his mouth like a zipper. "My lips are sealed."

Before Connor could push his brother further, he heard the sweet sound of Sienna's voice. During his weaker moments, he'd laid in bed at night replaying her voicemails until he couldn't handle it. There was something different though, seeing her all gussied up for the press. It was his girl, but this was the version she shared with the world.

Sienna looked gorgeous in a simple black dress that hugged her figure. Connor's hands literally itched to feel her curves again, to trace his fingers down the trail of freckles. Her dark hair was styled off her face, with waves hanging down her back. She was a vision; she was perfect.

Watching this interview was going to be torture. Watching it with Colby was going to be murder.

"Thanks for taking the time to talk with us," the interviewer said. Connor had seen the guy before; he was a network sports staple.

Sienna sat straight, her hands resting on her lap. She seemed totally at ease in the spotlight, and Connor was so proud of his Golden Girl. "Thanks for taking the time to meet with me." The pair bounced back basic Q&As for a moment, until they got to the question that Sienna had hinted at when they were at the lodge.

"So, let's talk about the future. Are these the last games for Sienna Markum?" The interviewer leaned forward, expecting a ratings-worthy reply. His veneers sparkled in the studio lighting. They looked like a mouthful of unchewed Chiclets.

Sienna licked her lips and smiled. "Yes, I believe they are. You see, skiing has been my life. I love it, don't get me wrong, but when a woman gets to a certain age, she starts to think about other things. She starts to wonder what's beyond the slopes." Her words brought a ball of fire to his stomach, and Connor had to focus on breathing.

Almost like he knew what was coming, Colby twitched.

The interviewer smirked. "Sounds like you have an announcement to make."

Sienna paused for a moment before turning to the camera. Her gray gaze bore through the screen, and Connor felt his stomach flip. "I do. No matter what happens this week, it will be my final competition."

The interviewer beamed, seemingly delighted with her response. "It is? And why is that?"

"You see, I've met someone."

Connor couldn't be certain, but he thought he heard Beverly yelp off-camera.

"So there's a man," the interviewer said with a sleazy wink. Connor made a mental note to punch the guy the next time he saw him. He'd wipe that smirk off his face and cost him a new set of teeth.

Sienna glanced to the side for a moment before continuing. "There is a man. He's brought a lot of joy to my life. Most importantly, he showed me I can be Sienna Markum, even if I'm not competing. I think it's time for the next chapter in my life." Sienna looked back to the camera and gave a sheepish grin. "That is, if he'll still have me."

Color drained from Connor's face at her declaration. The rushing sound in his ears nearly drowned out the sounds of Colby cheering beside him. His brother was now on his feet, whooping and jumping around the room like a lottery winner.

"What are you waiting for? Let's go get your girl."

Slowly, the pieces started to click into place. "You knew about this. How?"

Colby walked to the mini bar, pulled out two small bottles of vodka, and shrugged. "We bumped into each other last night before her interview and had a chat." He tossed one of the bottles to Connor before draining his. "Now drink up, you'll need your courage."

*

Sienna stood at the top of the mountain; the last mountain in competition. The air was cool and nipped at her skin, but she felt amazing. Win or lose, she knew she was doing the right thing. It was time to find a new purpose in life, and she hoped Connor would be a part of it.

After her interview, Colby convinced her that she did the right thing. He was certain that Connor would find her. Since the interview aired right before her final race, she had no idea when, or if, she would see him. The notion brought butterflies to her stomach, but she swallowed down the fear. Her heart was Connor's, and she knew he would come and claim it. She just needed to have faith.

The other thing Sienna knew for certain was her mother was stark raving mad. As soon as the cameras were off, she was at Sienna's side scolding her like a child. For the first time, and long overdue, Sienna turned to her mother and shrugged. "I'm done, Mom. It's time for me to move on."

Beverly had not taken the news well and alternated between sobbing and screaming at her daughter until that morning. Then she fell into silence that Sienna would have found impressive if it didn't annoy her so much.

Fearing she'd alienated both of her parents; Sienna was touched when her father found her. He rested his hands on her shoulders and kissed her temple. "I'm so proud of you, Sweetheart. No matter what, you're my champion."

"What about Mom?" she asked, hating that she still craved her approval.

"For once, let me worry about her." He nodded and gestured toward the waiting ski lift.

The judges came to the line and Sienna had two minutes until the start. She closed her eyes and took a calming breath. When she opened them, she saw everything clearly: the slopes and tracks ahead of her, the shine of her skis, and the clear sky. This was her moment, and she was going to take it.

As soon as she pushed off the block, Sienna knew this was her race to win. Her body felt one with the skis, effortlessly taking each hill and turning like a warm knife cutting through butter. Going into the finals, she had been in the points lead, so she would know instantly when she crossed the line if the gold was hers. Her heart pumped in her ears, but Sienna savored every turn. Knowing it was her last run made it bittersweet, but her soul told her it was the right decision.

Cresting the final hill, Sienna tucked in for the descent. The roar of the crowd echoed off the mountains, and she bit back a smile as her skis crossed the blue finish line. Sienna closed her eyes and listened to the sounds around her as she caught her breath. These were the cheers she'd remember more than any others. She'd earned each chant and shout of praise over the years, and she deserved the chance to savor the moment.

Through the cheers, Sienna thought she heard a familiar voice calling her name. Keeping her eyes closed, she pretended that Connor was here to see her. If Colby kept his word, she knew Connor would have seen her interview, would know how she felt. Turning around, she looked for the owner of the voice. As the sound of her name grew closer, Sienna knew it was him. Her eyes flew open, and she turned toward his voice.

"Connor?"

Breaking free of the crowd and pushing toward the barrier, Connor waved his arms in the air. He was dressed for winter, in a puffy red coat that matched the hue of his cold cheeks. His sandy hair was buried under a navy beanie that brought his blue eyes to life. Clutched in his hands, Connor held a homemade sign that read Sienna's #1 fan.

Sienna burst out laughing at the sweet gesture and skied toward him. The flash of cameras put stars in her eyes, but Sienna was focused only on Connor. When she made it to the barricade, Connor reached out and pulled her to him. Since her goggles were still on, they hit his forehead and blocked their lips.

Both of them laughed as he pulled the goggles free and

kissed her, right in front of the world. He cradled her close, or as close as her ski gear and the partition would allow, and ran his hand up and down her arms. His eyes sparkled as he took her in, and she'd never felt so treasured.

"I love you, Sienna." He breathed her name like a prayer in the cool, winter air.

"Connor, I'm so sorry, I—" He cut her off with another kiss. Finally, they came up for air and she took in his expression. There was tenderness and love in his eyes, and she knew that she would be looking into those eyes for the rest of her life.

"I love you, too."

Connor cupped her cheeks in his hands. "I'm so proud of you, my Golden Girl."

Only then did Sienna realize she hadn't looked at the scoreboard to confirm her ranking. "Did I win?" she blurted out, pulling away to see her score.

Connor chuckled, unable to hide his prideful expression. Her question was answered when she saw her name fill the screen—she'd won the gold medal. She wasn't sure how she was supposed to feel. After a lifetime of training and living with purpose, she suddenly had it all. After everything she'd been through, Sienna Markum was finally everyone's Golden Girl. And it was pretty damn magical.

EPILOGUE

Christmas, the following year

The lodge looked even better than it had the year before. Connor and Sienna were thrilled to be back, and this time on their own terms. When the games finished, Sienna had her gold medal, Connor had taken the bronze, and they had both found each other. No one was complaining about the outcomes.

Well, except maybe Beverly. The good news was that no one was overly interested in what she thought. How was that for freeing?

One surprise that came after the games was what happened with their careers. Karl opened a coaching school outside Aspen for aspiring skiers, primarily those looking to compete in the Paralympic games. He'd bought a share of the ski lodge and was looking for two assistant coaches to train the next generation. When it was time to create his coaching team, he knew just where to look with his most recent champions.

Connor and Sienna jumped at the opportunity and never looked back.

When the time came for them to find a place to live,

Sienna was delighted to discover that Connor found them a house near the lodge. They didn't have to travel far for work, and they were still within minutes of the slopes. Even better, their new place had a yard big enough for Roscoe to roam free. Her little rescue had fallen hard for Connor, and the feeling was mutual. It did her heart good to see her two favorite beings living in harmony.

Sienna and Connor sat on the balcony, settling in for a Christmas Eve just the two of them. After some serious bribery, Connor closed part of the lodge for just Sienna and him. He wanted to recreate the magic of the year before, and she wasn't about to argue. The tree was back in the lobby, albeit a lot larger and bursting with lights. They'd even hung a pair of stockings on the mantel, a small tradition that warmed Sienna. They were making new memories while savoring the old.

Perhaps the best part of the lodge's renovations was that the pool house was back in service. "You know," Sienna said, her fingers tracing lines up and down Connor's arm. He was wrapped around her and she basked in his proximity. "Since you closed down the west side of the lodge, there isn't anyone using the pool."

She felt Connor shake beside her, laughter bubbling up from his chest. "Why my word," he said with a chuckle. "Are you suggesting we christen the pool?"

Lowering her voice, she said, "I think you know I'm suggesting more than a quick dip."

To Sienna's disappointment, Connor didn't jump up and run toward the door. She thought the promise of skinny dipping would light a fire under her boyfriend.

"While that sounds like heaven on earth," Connor whispered into her ear, "I'm not quite done with this sunset." He pulled her close and Sienna turned to rest her head on his shoulder. The view was gorgeous, but even after all this time she couldn't get enough of Connor.

As the sun dipped below the horizon, Sienna stared into the fading twilight. The mountains sparkled around them, and she couldn't think of a more beautiful sight. "I think we'll need to spend every Christmas here," she said with a smile. It was a regular part of her day, this beaming grin. Sienna couldn't think of a time in the last year when she wasn't blissfully happy. If it wasn't happening to her, she probably wouldn't believe someone could be this deliriously in love.

"Twist my arm." Connor laughed, pulling her even tighter.

Last Christmas, Connor's Captain Christmas routine had blown her away. Sienna didn't know how he could improve on anything. "How can you make this Christmas better than our first?" Connor shifted beside her, inching free to stand next to her. She looked at him and laughed. "I didn't mean to offend you. I'm sure you have something amazing planned."

Careful of his prosthesis, Connor eased himself down to one knee. "It's funny you should mention surprises because I have one more for you." Sienna gasped as their eyes met, Connor's blue gaze glinting with affection. He retrieved a small box from his pocket and held it up to her. "Sienna, you have changed my life and given me a purpose I didn't know I needed. Every day is better because I get to spend it with you. Will you make me the happiest man in the world and marry me?"

Dissolving into a puddle of tears, Sienna pulled Connor to her and kissed him. "Of course I'll marry you." Her heart almost burst with happiness and pride at having this man in her life. For all her concerns about life after competition, she needn't have worried. There were a lot more adventures ahead.

"Oh thank God," he teased as he fumbled taking the ring out of the box.

"Now give me that ring," she teased.

Connor chuckled as he slid the gold ring onto her finger. The ring was custom designed, with three bands of gold wrapped together; reminiscent of the Paralympic emblem.

"And here you thought you were done collecting gold."

The End

A SNEAK PEEK AT ANOTHER ROMANCE BY LIBBY KAY

Chapter One

Ginny Meyer glanced at her phone for the third time in two minutes. Was time standing still? From her spot in the rental car line, she knew it would be another five minutes before she got to the front. An elderly woman in an ugly Christmas sweater perched on the edge of the counter, explaining all the reasons she couldn't drive a stick shift. Once again, Ginny looked at the time and grimaced. She promised her dad she'd be on the road an hour ago.

After taking a cleansing breath, Ginny took in her surroundings. Despite the fact that most people were still digesting their Thanksgiving leftovers, the rental store had already decked the halls. Piney wreaths hung in front of each kiosk, and tinny Christmas carols filtered through the overhead speakers. As a girl, Ginny had loved Christmas. The traditions, the presents, the cookies covered in edible glitter. Christmas brought back some of her favorite childhood memories.

Christmas also brought one of the most painful memories of her life. Especially since she was mere hours away from facing her past head-on. Nope, she would save the soul searching for Ohio. Right now, in New York, she had enough to handle, starting with the festive trouble maker in front of her.

"You see, dear," the woman said over the barrier at the kiosk, "I asked for a different car."

The clerk behind the desk bit her lip and forced a professional smile. "Yes, ma'am. As I said, we can give you a compact car, but it won't be in the evergreen color. All we have available is black."

The woman leaned back on her heels, as if driving a black car was grounds for a nervous breakdown. "But dear, it's Christmas time. I can't show up to Pennsylvania in something that isn't festive." To punctuate her point, she gestured down at her sweater.

Ginny stifled a groan as the clerk nodded and gestured for a manager to assist her. Ginny didn't see what all the fuss was about; a car was a car and who cared if it was green, black, or purple. Behind her, another customer cleared his throat and gestured at his watch with an expression that was anything but jolly. "We all have places to go," he mumbled just loud enough for the older woman to hear.

Pulling herself to her full height of barely five feet, the older woman stomped back to the man and pointed with a gnarled finger. "Young man, I would appreciate some patience and kindness. You will get your turn as soon as I'm finished. There's no need to be rude this close to Christmas." She nodded at her words and turned before he could respond. Ginny hazarded a glance over her shoulder and saw the man was as red as the woman's sweater. Apparently, no one wants to get scolded by Mrs. Claus in public.

GET YOUR OWN COPY....
AVAILABLE WHERE BOOKS ARE SOLD...

ACKNOWLEDGEMENTS

To the team at Inkspell—especially Melissa, Shel, and Yeza—you make me feel like a literary rockstar. Thank you for all your help, guidance, and support.

To the late, great Dianne Drake—thank you for pointing me in the right direction with my writing. You took me under your wing, and I'll never forget your guidance. Thank you.

To Teri McGill, who read this story first and gave me the confidence to keep writing. Thank you.

A shout out to the Hemingway to my Fitzgerald—thank you for making my time during "funemployment" so magical. I'll always treasure our literary lunches.

Last, but certainly not least, to my family and friends. Your faith in my writing has made me the person I am today—for better or worse. 😊

Love you all!

ABOUT THE AUTHOR

Libby Kay lives in the city in the heart of the Midwest with her husband. When she's not writing, Libby loves reading romance novels of any kind. Stories of people falling in love nourish her soul. Contemporary or Regency, sweet or hot, as long as there is a happily ever after she's in love!

When not surrounded by books, Libby can be found baking in her kitchen, binging true crime shows, or on the road with her husband, traveling as far as their bank account will allow.

Writing is a solitary job, and Libby loves to hear from readers. Reach out and review her stories anytime. She'd love to hear from you.

Website: https://www.libbykayauthor.com/
Facebook: @LibbyKayAuthor
Goodreads: Libby Kay
Instagram:
https://www.instagram.com/libbykayauthor/

Bookbub: https://www.bookbub.com/profile/libby-kay

Made in the USA
Monee, IL
09 March 2023

29509293R00069